Their touch was electric. It sizzled along his arm, infecting the rest of his body so fast he gasped.

Do you see? she whispered mysteriously, her green eyes bewitching him and beckoning him closer and closer, until their lips met.

And suddenly her substance, which he'd thought he'd found lacking, hit him in the chest like a blow from a club. It heated his blood and made his knees start to wobble. Matthew closed his eyes and gave himself up to their kiss.

Their kiss was far more than just a peck; it was much, much more than was improper; it was enough to send them both charging immediately into societal exile. . . .

By Patricia Wynn
Published by Fawcett Books:

THE BUMBLEBROTH
A COUNTRY AFFAIR
THE CHRISTMAS SPIRIT

THE CHRISTMAS SPIRIT

Patricia Wynn

FAWCETT CREST • NEW YORK

A Fawcett Crest Book
Published by Ballantine Books
Copyright © 1996 by Patricia Wynn Ricks

All rights reserved under International and Pan-American Copyright Conventions. Published in the United States by Ballantine Books, a division of Random House, Inc., New York, and simultaneously in Canada by Random House of Canada Limited, Toronto.

http://www.randomhouse.com

Library of Congress Catalog Card Number: 96-96578

ISBN: 0-449-22520-8

Manufactured in the United States of America

First Edition: November 1996

10 9 8 7 6 5 4 3 2 1

To Father Christmas
and all his elves

At Drontheim, Olaf the King
Heard the bells of Yule-tide ring,
　　As he sat in his banquet-hall,
Drinking his nut-brown ale,
With his bearded Berserks hale
　　And tall.

O'er his drinking horn, the sign
He made of the Cross divine
　　As he drank, and muttered his prayers;
But the Berserks evermore
Made the sign of the Hammer of Thor
　　Over theirs.

　　　　　　Longfellow, *King Olaf's Christmas*

Chapter One

He only used to see me, ye know, when the fever was upon him. That's why he thought I was not real.

Sir Matthew Dunstone was his name, and the story I'm tellin' ye about him is true, as sure as I'm standin' here right now.

It happened long ago at the Yuletide, the season they like to call Christmas, though at that time not many folks put their faith in Christmas or in stories told by elves. But that is just what this is, ye see, a tale as is told by me, Francis the elf.

Now, for the year an' a bit before he first seen me, Sir Matthew would sit all alone in front of his fire for most of his days and on into his every evenin'. He was still a youngish man, but the disease he'd picked up in them heathenish places he'd explored—the ones he used to rant about in his dreams—had wrecked his poor body as well as his mind. His frame had been much sturdier once, I could see, and his face beneath that dark, wavy hair of his had a yellowish tint that he'd not been born with. His cheeks were all lean and hollowlike, with a great, nasty scar comin' near to his mouth. So that when he'd stare at me in the dim light of his fire, nearly all I could see of 'im was a pair of dark, gleaming eyes.

The first time I seen 'im, I was sittin' in a fine old oak tree in the mews right outside his library window, just the kind of oak us elves likes to play in. It was autumn, I believe, and the leaves were all crimson and goldlike, and I was giving this tree a bit of a try-on when I spied him ahuddled there near his fire. He had a strange sort o' glitter to his eyes. A look as if to mean that he was seein' things he'd rather not see. His face was glistening, too, but not from the coal fire at his feet as much as from the heat in his body that made him shiver.

And he was talkin' to himself.

Now, ye will think, as I did, that Sir Matthew must've been tipplin' just a wee bit too much, but he hadn't touched so much as a drop of wine with his dinner, as I later saw. We elves like to tease a fellow when he's in his cups. Else I never would have shown meself to him.

But there he was, amutterin' to himself and lookin' as if he was keeping himself in his seat by the strength in them long, narrow fingers o' his. So, I says to meself, he must be three sheets to the wind— prime game for an elf—so I slipped right quick inside his window like and perched up on the mantelpiece.

And very glad to see me he was, though it took a bit o' dancin' on me part to get his attention. He was havin' one o' them dreams, ye know, the kind in which the shadows of yer past come back to haunt ye. And given Sir Matthew's past, what with all them terrible things he'd seen, a fair horror his *dreams must've been. So that when he yanked himself out o' them all suddenlike and saw me prancin' there on his chimneypiece, he was just that glad it was me.*

Now, if I had known then what was agoin' to happen, I'd have stayed far away from that tree and never visited Sir Matthew no more, but I didn't, ye see, so this was how it happened. . . .

"Francis . . ."

Matthew tried to speak through his shivering teeth, a difficult task, even though his tremors had eased as soon as he'd seen the elf, the small, wizened creature dressed all in green that was the product of his hallucinations. As he had done for the past few weeks, ever since he had first imagined this illusive figure, Matthew focused all his will on the grinning elf—impossibly seated on the narrow chimneypiece—so as not to slip back into those other, more terrifying delusions. The ones in which slaves and whip-wielding slavers, warring tribes and bloodthirsty chieftains battled for his soul.

"Francis"—he strove for a normal conversational note, not that of a raving, feverish man—"Francis, I wonder why, if I had to invent an elf, I did not give you a different sort of name?"

"And what sort o' name would that be?" Francis asked, jutting out his beard as if he'd just been insulted.

It was astonishing really, Matthew thought, just how logical their conversations always seemed to be. Statement followed question or vice versa, just as they did in real life. Whereas in his other

3

dreams, the genuine nightmares, all the images ran together, producing a greater horror than the horrors he had lived.

At the thought of those other hallucinations, a phantom memory snaked into Matthew's mind, bringing shudders in its wake. He gripped the sturdy arms of his chair.

"What is it, laddie?" Francis's sharp voice dragged him back from the brink of a deep, yawning pit. "Has the devil got yer tail?"

"Yes." Matthew responded with an effort, bringing his gaze back to the welcome face in front of him. "But no matter—where were we?"

Francis crossed his legs in midair and folded his arms across his chest. "You were mumblin' some nonsense about me name."

"Oh, yes, I remember now. I was wondering why I had not named you something more appropriate. Something like Prospero."

A grimace of profound disgust rolled over the elf's features. "Prospero? Now, who the devil would he be? One of yer heathens, then?"

If he could have laughed, Matthew would have, but when he was shivering so, the effort was always much too great. All he could manage was the ghost of a smile. "No, he's a wizard from Shakespeare. I am disappointed in myself," he said, "for conjuring a companion who hasn't read him."

"Now, there ye go again, ye scurvy rascal," Francis growled. "Sayin' as how ye've invented me, when the fact is, me parents did just fine without yer help. What gives ye the bloody gall to think ye had anything to do with the makin' o' me?"

4

"I'm not at all certain," Matthew confessed. A fresh surge of fever had suddenly swept through him, pulling the clouds in front of his eyes, so that even Francis seemed far away and moving farther still. "Sometimes I'm not certain of anything." A wave of shivering spread through his whole body and up to his head. All his limbs started to ache.

"Heating up again, are ye, laddie? Want me to call that grim-faced giant ye call a manservant?"

"In a minute." Matthew shook his head, trying to clear the fog away. Ahmad was not his servant, actually—more in the nature of a bodyguard. Matthew was ashamed when he had to call him, but there were times when he could not walk without the strength in Ahmad's arm. And Matthew had to acknowledge that it was far easier to help a conscious man to his room, however weak he might be, than to pick an unconscious one off the floor.

But the mist was lifting again, and pale green eyes under a black set of brows were peering down at him from a wizened face.

"You are very considerate, you know," Matthew managed quite sincerely. "Not at all what one would expect from an elf. Before meeting you, I had thought that elves were all troublemakers."

"I've already told ye, laddie, them are the other kind. The trolls. The kind what lives in caves." Francis gave a delicate shudder. "Ugly they are."

"Unlike you?"

Matthew's irony did not escape Francis. "Here!" he said, drawing himself up. "Yer no great beauty yerself. Have ye taken a peek in the mirror lately?"

"Only to shave. But it was hardly necessary. You

don't have to tell me I've lost whatever attraction I had for women. Though even if I hadn't..." Matthew let his sentence drop off. It had not mattered what his appearance had been when he'd returned from his explorations. Helen had already forsaken her promise and married someone else.

But he refused to let his thoughts dwell upon that treachery. Such memories only led to bitterness, which exacerbated his fever.

"So these elves who live in caves are uglier than you?" He strove to keep to the conversation, however imaginary. "They must be quite remarkable."

Francis acknowledged this with a vigorous nod. "It's not just their men, ye see. It's their ladyfolk, too, whereas ours are fairer than the moonbeams. Ye've not heard how beautiful the elf maidens are?"

"If I had, I suppose I should have invented one of them instead of you."

"There ye go again, ye wretch, speakin' o' things ye can't understand. But I'll forgive ye this time since yer sick and ravin' like. I'll even give ye a treat and tell ye about me sister, Gertrude."

"Gertrude?" Matthew closed his eyes and muttered to himself, "Wherever do I get these names," before he asked, "She couldn't be Ariel or Ariadne, I don't suppose?"

Francis folded his arms and gave Matthew a quelling glare. "No, she couldn't. She's got the name our mother give her, and I'll bloody thank ye to leave it that way."

"If you insist."

"Well, do ye want to hear about her or no?"

"Should I?"

"Yes. And if ye saw her, ye wouldn't be asking such a foolish question." A curious pride seemed to puff Francis's chest. "Our Gertrude, now there's a pretty lass. As beautiful as the sunlight in the glen, she is. And can she dance! As light as the mist on a fern leaf. Though ye mustn't think," he quickly added, "that she's as flighty as some of yer sillier girls. Not our Trudy." He paused to consider, and a surprised look came over his features. "As a matter of fact," he said, "she's a bit like you."

"Like me?" Matthew raised his head to focus better on the elf. "In what way?"

Francis nodded smugly. "Now I see I've got yer interest. Well, I'll tell ye," he said, "though ye don't deserve to know. Our Trudy's a world traveler, she is."

"Really? Where has she been?"

"All them places ye talk about and more. She can circle the globe faster than the sun, so she can."

Matthew let his head drop back against his chair. At times his own ravings amazed him, but on this occasion, a nagging pain in his chest gave reason to his illusions. Not that he would ever admit this to a living soul, but he had been so lonely of late.

As his bitter anger over Helen's defection had waned, a much deeper ache had taken its place. The sheer misery of a man who's been robbed of a woman and, at the same time, of all likelihood of ever finding another.

So it was no surprise, really, that his hallucinations should take this tack. What amused him was the absurd formality of them. He sighed.

"What do I have to do," he said, "to meet this Trudy of yours? Beg an introduction?"

"Sure, and that would be a good place to start."

But Sir Matthew didn't beg. Even with a fever upon him that was shakin' his whole body, Sir Matthew had his limits, and a proud and stubborn man he could be. I could see that the talk about our Trudy had captured his interest, but he was never a man to let his feelings show. He'd been disappointed, he said, in the fickleness of women, so he had no further interest, said he, in the fairer sex. And I took him at his word, ye see, though I shouldn't have. . . .

So Trudy came, and a pretty sight she was, asittin' up in the tree beside me on a cold wintry evening when the stars were all atwinkling like a million fairy lights. Her short, black hair gleamed in the dark like a piece of glossy coal, shimmering blue on green, and her pale green eyes cheered my heart like the sight of an English meadow. . . .

"There." Francis pointed through the window at the man in his dressing gown.

Trudy bent from her perch on the barren twig to see. The sight that met her eyes caused a sudden pause in her heartbeat, for the man looked so alone. A book lay open on his lap, but he was not reading it. His head lay back against the chair, his eyelids pinched tightly against the light. His face appeared gaunt, and the lines in his cheeks reflected deprivation. A scar, freshly healed, ran from his cheekbone to the corner of his mouth.

"That's Sir Matthew?" she said, pulling herself up to join her brother on his frozen limb.

"Aye, he's the one I've been tellin' ye about. An' a right poor devil he is."

"What's made him sick?"

"All that gallivantin' to India and Africa—all them places ye shouldn't be caught in neither, as I've told ye and told ye—"

" 'Time and again,' I know," Trudy teased. "Though that's nonsense. As if I could be caught by a disease!"

"No, but ye might be trapped by one o' them heathens and put into an iron cage, as I've heard they do if they catch one of their jinn."

"As if I would let meself get trapped! Ye just don't want me to go away from home, now do ye?"

"And what's wrong with staying here, where ye belong?" Francis grumbled. "Ye can't tell me them foreign places have any fancier spots to dance than we do. I'd like to see a prettier sight than a Scottish hillock or an English meadow."

Trudy sighed. She couldn't explain why she felt such a restlessness to travel, or why the simple dances and pranks of her fellow elves left her feeling incomplete. "I just like to wander, I suppose."

Turning to the matter at hand, she added, "But tell me more about Sir Matthew. Why did ye call me?"

"I think he'd do a mite better for a wee bit o' female company." Francis gave her a wink. "I thought some o' yer antics might make him forget his troubles. I've tried all o' mine."

"What sort of troubles are they?"

"Well—" Francis settled himself in the crook of the tree and leaned comfortably against its trunk.

To any person below he would have seemed but a cluster of mistletoe, with his green felt for leaves, his beard for stems, and his pearly buttons for berries. But Trudy could see him clearly. His little round eyes twinkled back at her, and the nose on his tiny face, which was uncommonly large, twitched when he spoke, putting her in mind of an exotic monkey that had once made her laugh.

"Near as I can make out," Francis began, crossing his legs at the knee, "Sir Matthew did himself in, asearchin' for the source o' the Nile. Made him a baronet, they did, after his first trip. Though why any grown man would care to know where a muddy old river springs from fair has me bamboozled."

His wrinkled brow posed her a question that Trudy was at pains to answer.

"I can't tell ye why a man would care to know that sort of thing," she said. "With me, it's not the knowing, so much as the searching, so that when I get there all the pleasure I've promised meself slips right away, and so I'm off again on another search.

"But is that all that ails him?" she asked. "Just a spot of fever and some beasties in his stomach?" She was sure there must be more, even though she knew the horrors such a journey posed for someone no stronger than a human. Most Britishers who set out to find the secrets of the African rivers never returned.

"No." Francis grimaced. "It's not so much his body what ails him, though that's considerable. It's what goes on in that head of his. He must've had a fright or two along the way, bad enough to scare the soul right out of him."

"Poor mannie!" Trudy bent down again to have another peek at Matthew.

His eyes were open now, and he had straightened himself to call a manservant into the room, a great, tall man with fair skin and thick black eyebrows, dressed in the white tunic and baggy pants of a Pathan warrior. A huge white turban circled his head, making him seem that much larger, though he must have stood well over six feet with his head bare.

As big as the Pathan was, Sir Matthew managed to look strong and broad-shouldered beside him. A strange feeling constricted Trudy's chest when she saw him decline the use of his servant's arm. She had no doubt he was feeling weak, but he held himself proudly as he was escorted from the room. The Pathan held back, ready to catch Matthew if he fell. Trudy wondered what act had bound these men together, for the Pathans were an independent race, not likely to hire on as any man's servant. This she had seen on her travels, as well as the strange bonds that sometimes formed between men. There had been times when she had envied them that bond she could not understand.

But Matthew did not seem to be a candidate for envy at the moment, though the square set of his shoulders protected him equally from her pity. Any sympathy she felt had to be tempered by the respect due a man who had endured the hardships he must have experienced: hunger and heat, exhaustion and disease, the treachery of sworn friends, the predations of brigands, danger from tyrants who mistrusted any foreigner, and the assault of cruelty upon cruelty on his eyes and his mind.

Yes, Sir Matthew needed some distraction from the memories she could imagine all too well. Yet, as Trudy watched him leave the room, a vague disquiet came over her, provoked by her brother's uncommon silence.

"Why," she said, facing Francis, "why do I detect a hint of scheming? Ye've never wanted me to reveal meself to a man before."

"But this one's helpless with his fever," Francis explained, grinning. "And besides, Sir Matthew's sworn off women, or so he says, and he don't intend to be pixie-led. Bit of a challenge, wouldn't ye say, to see if he can resist a beauty such as yerself?"

A moment's pause, and Francis's eyes lit up with mischief. "What say, sister, if I lay ye a bet that ye can't lure him into the mists before Christmas?"

"Lure him into the mists? In his condition? I thought ye felt sorry for him."

"And so I do. But ye can't think I'd let me sister near a man like him if he weren't in such sorry straits. I know all humans are fools, but that's not to say ye can fool the lot o' them."

Trudy rolled her eyes. "And ye think it's yer job to keep me safe? Have I told ye, yer a relic from the Dark Ages, ye are? Do ye have any idea what I've been up to while I was away?"

"Ye've mentioned a thing or two before." Francis scowled. "But if I've got ye here, doin' yer bit to trick Sir Matthew, then I can keep me eyes on you as well. And if ye do lead him on a pretty chase, wisp that ye are, I'm sure ye wouldn't hurt him any worse than he is already. If I were a human, I'd a lot rather dance me way to elfland than sit by a fire, feeling me bones rot right out of me body."

"A lot you'd know what humans feel!"

"Same as yerself! Yer as soulless as me!"

It was true that she was, and yet Trudy resented this particular taunt. Somehow she was sure she knew more about humans than her brother did. She never had shared the contempt for them her fellow elves held, and sometimes her wanderings had taken her perilously close to their world.

But she had never come too close. She'd avoided that ultimate encounter with men, with its attendant danger to rob her of all her magic. That had not prevented her, however, from skipping in the air in front of them, just out of reach, to lead men who'd been lost in the desert to water, or from causing a flurry of chaos in a slave caravan in the hope that some of the slaves would escape. And it would not keep her now from doing what she could to help Sir Matthew find a way out of his despair and into the mists.

Something about his stiff, retreating figure had intrigued her. She couldn't help wondering if an explorer such as he had suffered from the same sort of restlessness she had known, and if he understood what it was. All Trudy knew was that her wanderings rarely brought her any satisfaction, though she was sure that to stay at home doing nothing more than what the other elves did would only be worse.

"Ye say that Sir Matthew never goes out?" she asked Francis, musing.

"Not that I've ever seen. He just sits in that chair

o' his, most of the time, he does, except when he's sleeping."

Trudy frowned and tapped her chin with one finger. "Then no wonder his memories trouble him so. He needs something new to take their place."

"That's the spirit! I knew ye'd jump at a challenge. But I'm warnin' ye, Trudy, Sir Matthew'll be a hard nut to crack."

Trudy scoffed. "I'll have him eating out of me hand and in elfland before Christmas, sure enough. Just ye wait and see."

And that was what I did, though I should've noticed right then and there that she had something addlepated in mind. I should've known by the way she stared at Sir Matthew and the light flickered in her eyes. But I didn't, ye see, or I would've stopped her before the whole thing got out of hand, and a terrible tragedy would have been averted. But that's our Trudy for ye. She always did do things her own way, with no proper reflection beforehand.

And as for Sir Matthew ... Well, that's the last time I'll believe any man who claims he won't be pixie-led.

Chapter Two

*T*rudy stood before the front door of Sir Matthew's lodgings in Gilbert Street and, before knocking, took a moment to survey her appearance. Beneath her elfin cloak was a simple white muslin gown with tiny pink posies worked into the cloth. The pale green color of their leaves picked up the meadow green of her eyes, and the lively pink of the flowers matched the perpetual bloom in her cheeks. She was very pleased to think she had conjured the gown all by herself. The fact that the dress was merely an illusion did nothing to dull the thrill of wearing it. She was sure she had perfectly dressed the part of a fashionable lady of the ton.

Her rapid tap with the knocker was not immediately answered, but she reminded herself that humans were excruciatingly slow in everything. While she waited, she contented herself with the keen anticipation of entering their world as one of their own. What Francis would say when he discovered her plan, she did not know, but she could almost see the blood rising into his cheeks right now. She would lure Sir Matthew into the mists well before

Christmas, but first she meant to have a little adventure of her own.

The door opened slowly. The Pathan warrior she had spied through the window these past few nights filled the entryway and dwarfed her fragile self. At the sight of her beauty—much as she had done to hide its otherworldliness—his eyes grew wide beneath their pair of heavy brows, but he soon recovered his dignity.

He bowed wordlessly after his Eastern fashion and waited for her to speak.

"Is this the lodging of Sir Matthew Dunstone?" she inquired in her acquired society voice.

The Pathan inclined his head, but his eyes never left her face.

"Would you tell him, please, that he has a visitor?"

The Pathan hesitated only a second before surprising her. "Sir Matthew does not receive," he said with a regretful bow. "He is unwell." And with that briefest of statements, he closed the door.

Trudy stared in disbelief at the flat, painted surface. She had never been refused to her face before. She wondered briefly if the problem was with the dress, if she had somehow failed to give the appearance of a respectable caller.

But as she looked down again, she could only nod approvingly. She liked the way the skirt subtly sparkled with the scattering of fairy dust she had added for trim. The innovation was her own, not strictly in the pattern books, but she did not think it enough of a departure to make a man take offense. Gentlemen were notoriously ignorant where female fashions were concerned, and besides, she wasn't quite prepared to give up all her advantages. An elf maid must attend to her attractions, same as any girl.

Having worked out her frustration in this idle musing, she returned to the problem at hand. She had intended to meet Sir Matthew entirely upon his own human terms, but if those failed, she was quite prepared to use magic, just as long as whatever trick she pulled could easily be explained. The big Pathan would be a formidable obstacle to any other girl, but he was as nothing to her.

Wrapping herself completely in her elfin cloak, she knocked again, letting her taps fall more heavily on the door to disguise their origin.

This time when the Pathan opened the door, she saw his blank stare of confusion. His brows snapped together darkly as he walked right past her and out into the street to peer this way and that. Assured that she was completely invisible to him, Trudy tip-toed daintily through the door, relieved to find that he had not been born on a Sunday. Those born on a Sunday had a remarkable gift for seeing elves, but since he obviously had not been, her task would be all the easier.

She waited until he had reentered, scratching the back of his head below his turban, then followed him up the stairs to a door near the landing. Judging by its position in the house, she had no doubt it was the door to Sir Matthew's library.

As the Pathan knocked and entered, her heart gave a leap of anticipation.

"Ahmad, who was at the door?"

Out in the corridor Trudy heard Matthew speak

for the first time and was astonished by the depth of his voice. She had not expected a seriously ill man to produce such a resonant tone, but Matthew's words filled the air with a low vibrancy, betraying none of the weakness his illness implied.

"It was a lady, Matthew saab," the Pathan answered. "She asked to see you."

"A lady? For me?" A hint of anxiety entered his voice.

Trudy tensed to learn its meaning, but all Matthew said next was, "Did she leave her card?"

"No, saab"—Ahmad's questioning tone revealed that he must have been more disconcerted by her presence than he had shown—"I am afraid I did not think to ask her."

"No matter. It was not—"

"No, saab." The Pathan's voice softened but a notch. "It was not the memsaab."

The silence that followed his statement made Trudy squirm with a rare uneasiness. Though she couldn't see Matthew, she somehow sensed his embarrassment.

But all he said when he did resume speaking as lightly as before was, "I cannot imagine that it would be, but neither can I think of any other lady who might call. Must have been an error."

"Yes, undoubtedly, saab."

Trudy waited for some time after Ahmad had withdrawn before lifting her hand to the knob. Matthew's acceptance of her story would depend very much upon her timing.

"Sir Matthew?" She pushed the door open with a

18

falsely timid knock, making sure not to speak so early as to have her entrance denied.

As she advanced into the room, he looked up, startled, and instantly his brows snapped together over a lean, haggard face. Then as her beauty, fully released, struck him with powerful force, his lips parted and all time seemed to suspend.

Trudy had meant to use these moments of enchantment to satisfy her own curiosity. But her study became not so much a conscious design as a mirror of Matthew's wonder.

She had seen many men before. She had observed them all her life in countless situations, but none had struck her with the sheer force of character that Matthew did. He was free of his ague today. She had purposely waited until his last bout of malaria had passed, knowing she would not be received if he was genuinely ill.

Now she wondered how even that dreaded disease, which affected all who traveled in the Tropics, could keep such a strong man pinned to his chair. Determination seemed to reside in the long cut of Matthew's jaw. Mental energy issued from his deep, dark eyes, betraying the lightning quickness of a profound intellect. Even dazed as he was by her magic, he seemed to see right through to her very core.

Trudy wondered nervously if perhaps Francis had not underestimated the strength of their mark.

But then even as she stood there, other details about him worked their own fascination, so that Trudy forgot for a moment her purpose in coming. His hair had the rich, wavy texture of meadow grass, the kind that made her want to sink her toes right in. His forehead was prominent over a set of well-defined eyebrows. And even with the ravagement of illness on his face and the scar, which made her cringe from the savagery that had caused it, she couldn't miss the fact that he was a stunningly handsome man.

A man she would like to lure into the mists, to place at her feet, and to feed with her own hand.

Surprisingly, Matthew was the first to break the trance that had fallen between them.

"Who the devil are you?" he said with a spare shake of his head, as if to clear a momentary dizziness.

Trudy gave a similar start. "I am Faye," she said without thinking.

A sudden glimmer lit his eyes. "Are you?" he asked, before muttering to himself, "Yes, I might believe you were if I was dreaming."

Confused and flustered by her lack of control in a situation designed by herself, Trudy bobbed him a hasty curtsy. "Forgive me. I should have said, I am Miss Faye Meriwether."

"That would have been much more proper, certainly. It does not explain, however, what a young, unescorted girl is doing by barging into my library, which is most definitely *im*proper."

"Nonsense!" Trudy was piqued that he thought of propriety when most men dreamed of ravishment when they glimpsed her. "I am much older than I look. As old as you, I daresay. And I have it upon the greatest authority, Sir Matthew, that you are younger than thirty."

"My age has nothing to do with it. How do you come to be in my library?"

Trudy had prepared herself for this question. With the practice of her race, she let the lie fall glibly from her tongue. "Ah, yes, well, I hope you will excuse me. But, you see, I did knock once and ask to speak to you. However, your manservant said you were not receiving visitors, so I started to go. . . .

"Then"—she feigned a lively astonishment—"without so much as a word, your man appeared to have a change of heart, for he opened the door again and stepped aside.

"I do not know what was in his mind," she added with a pensive frown, "for he did not speak, but taking his action for an invitation, I entered and waited to be shown to some withdrawing room to await your pleasure. I was left to cool my heels downstairs until I thought he must have forgotten all about me.

"Perhaps I should simply have gone away, but that would have been very cowardly of me, don't you think? So, I came in search of you. I hope you do not mind too dreadfully." Trudy gave him what she knew was a bewitchingly hopeful smile.

Instead of looking bewitched as she had hoped, Matthew seemed more than a bit suspicious. His eyes had narrowed.

"You will not mind if I ask my companion to join us, will you? And, by the way, he is my companion, not my manservant, as you've assumed."

"Not at all," Trudy said, raising her chin proudly. "Let him be called if you doubt my story."

Her offended air did nothing to dissuade him. Matthew leaned from his chair to ring the bell.

While they waited, he did seem to feel that some explanation of his rudeness was warranted. "You must forgive me for not rising," he said, his eyes growing darker as he perused her. "I have been very ill of late. It costs me much to stand."

"But, of course," Trudy said, though her heart sank to hear him. If he was truly that weak, her present plan would never work.

The seconds ticked between them, punctuated by a clock on the shelf. As they passed, Matthew seemed to forget himself long enough to stare at her strangely.

"Tell me, Miss Faye Meriwether," he said, and he seemed to probe his own mind for the answer. "Do you believe in second sight?"

Caught off guard, she stalled. "Pardon me?"

"In second sight. The power to see into the future."

"Oh, yes. That. Well—" Trudy's mind worked rapidly. "As a proper member of the Church, I should say no, shouldn't I?"

Matthew's lips quirked. "Undoubtedly."

"Then why do you ask?"

"It's nothing important." He gave his head a brisk shake. "Only that if I did believe in it, I would swear that I—"

He was interrupted by the door's opening.

"Saab?"

Ahmad's question preceded him, but when he caught sight of Trudy, he stepped quickly back. His eyes betrayed a start much akin to fright.

"Ahmad, this young lady says you refused her admittance, then reopened the door to let her pass."

"No, saab," Ahmad hotly denied it before Trudy turned her eyes on his with full force. His hazel gaze seemed to waver before hers when he said more hesitantly, "That is, I did open the door again, saab, but I did not see her. I thought I had heard another knocking."

"You did not see her enter the house?"

"No, saab." Ahmad blinked his eyes once, then twice. "I did not notice the young lady."

Trudy gazed back at Matthew, who was frowning. But all he said was, "Thank you, Ahmad. I shall not disturb you again. Not, at least, until Miss Meriwether requires your assistance from this house."

Ahmad made a deep salaam and closed the door, confusion still on his face.

"Strange—" A question clouded Matthew's sharp gaze. "Ahmad has the eyesight of an eagle. He can spot an enemy on a mountainside hundreds of yards away."

"Well, I am not your enemy, so perhaps that explains it." Trudy allowed a note of offense to enter her voice. Matthew *would* keep her standing in the middle of his room, and even she knew that was not a polite way to treat a lady caller. Any other gentleman would have fallen on his face to welcome such a pretty visitor to his rooms. "May I take a chair?" she asked haughtily.

"Certainly." Matthew emerged from his trance. "Please make yourself comfortable while you tell me what in blazes you are doing here."

His cutting tone did nothing to put her at ease. He was still on his guard. Trudy saw she would have to do more to win his confidence.

As she sat, she donned an expression of reluctance, and a shade of becoming honesty. "Very well, I will confess. . . . Sir Matthew, I'm afraid your companion startled me. He is so remarkably big, and—I almost hate to say it—his appearance is rather fierce. When he opened the door the second time, I suppose I cringed in a shadow, so he did not see me. And since he did not, I thought it would be much easier to slip in to see you, and once that was done, of course, I truly had intended to gird my loins, as the saying goes, to request a moment of your time, but he charged up the stairs and I never saw him again.

"So—" She took a deep breath, relieved to see that her lie was working. Matthew's brows had taken on a less cynical tilt, and Trudy continued, "You can see what happened, and I do apologize for being so forward, but when you hear what I have come about, you will understand that I acted out of the most selfless intentions."

"Just what did you come about, now that this misunderstanding has been cleared up?"

Trudy leaned forward in her chair and let her charm loose on Matthew. Musical tones fluttered from her lips. "I have come on the matter of gravest urgency for a number of poor unfortunates. I am hoping you will help me."

Suspicion and a hint of hostility on his part raised a shield that blocked her charm. "Please explain what you mean."

Trudy wondered if she might not have overplayed the part of the ingenue, when a more mature character might be needed here. She straightened her spine.

"I have come on behalf of the Society for the Relief of Indigent African Natives. We have established an almshouse near Tottenham Court Road here in London, and we are sorely in need of new subscribers."

A look of pure disbelief came into Matthew's eyes. A hint of amusement curved his lips. "Yes . . ." he said. "Go on."

"And . . ." she tried. But Matthew's amusement had had a most disconcerting effect. How dare he laugh at her?

"I assure you, Sir Matthew," Trudy said, drawing herself up in her seat to her full, diminutive height, "that the needs of our inmates are no laughing matter."

"I was not laughing at your inmates," he said, irritation overcoming his brief amusement. "I am quite certain they must be miserable. As miserable, in fact, as an Englishman who's been stranded in their country."

"Then, what were you smiling at?"

"At the notion that your so-called society would send an infant such as you to beg for funds."

Trudy's pride suffered a blow. "To beg? I do not beg. Nor am I an infant, Sir Matthew, as I have already informed you."

"So you have, and you have already proven your courage by sneaking into this house." Sir Matthew's gaze once again betrayed his suspicions. "Since when, however, have respectable English maids been sent alone into gentlemen's houses to solicit anything? Particularly remarkably pretty maids?"

Trudy didn't know whether to take this as a compliment or not. Certainly his final words had made the blood rush to her cheeks with a surprising intensity, as if she'd never heard pretty words before, when, in fact, she'd received a number of handsome compliments, all given with much greater enthusiasm than his. Perhaps her extreme reaction was due to her first impression that Matthew was completely impervious to her charms, so that she was more than just a little pleased to discover she was wrong. But whatever the reason, she now found herself at a loss for words.

A quite uncustomary sensation for an elf. As an unfamiliar thrill coursed through Trudy, she could almost believe that she was human.

"Well?" Matthew's deep voice prodded her insistently.

Trudy took refuge in dignity. She held her chin in the air. "I do not perfectly understand what you are implying, Sir Matthew."

"Do you not? Well, perhaps that is because I do not mean to imply anything at all. I cannot help wondering, however. Where are your parents? And why are you not at least chaperoned?"

"I"—Trudy's powers of invention rose to the occasion—"I do not choose to be chaperoned. Both my parents are dead, and I do as I please."

"You flaunt the conventions?" He arched one brow. "How very brave of you, indeed. What would they say about this at Almack's?"

"I do not waste my time at Almack's, so whatever

they say does not concern me. I am not as flighty as some of your sillier girls."

Matthew's forehead wrinkled with a sudden consternation. "What was that you said?" Something about her words seemed to have disturbed him.

She answered, "Merely that I have more important things to worry about. Such as the fate of our inmates. May we return to our discussion of them, please?"

He had been staring at her as if she had mysteriously echoed some thought inside his head, but now he gave it another shake and begged her to continue. In that minute, however, something had changed, and she could see that she was tiring him.

"If," she said hurriedly, "I might make a suggestion?" She rushed on without his assent. "If you would consider visiting the house our society has provided, you could see for yourself how desperate is our need for subscribers, and I am sure you would want to do something for our pensioners."

Matthew studied her from the depths of his chair. "What makes you sure?" he asked wearily. "Why have you come to me? My fortune is not so remarkable. I am a younger son, in fact. And"—he made a disparaging grimace at the brocaded robe he wore—"it is highly unlikely that I shall be doing anything to increase it."

"But you have been to Africa! You are one of the few members of society who has. Who else but you would care to help its people here?"

"Who else, indeed? Who but a madman?" His eyes narrowed again. "Weren't you told, Miss Faye Meriwether, that I had gone mad?"

Trudy blinked. In truth, his conversation had taken a decidedly odd turn. But no matter that Matthew's gaze had fixed on her with a disturbing, dark intensity, she did not feel afraid. Briefly she even wondered whether he might not be trying to frighten her.

"No," she said, shaking her head matter-of-factly. "I had not heard any such poppycock."

"Then you truly must have removed yourself from society, or you would have."

Matthew started to rise. Without thinking, Trudy leapt up to help him, but he stopped her with a glance.

She paused with her hand poised just below his elbow. He looked down on her from his great height, and all of a sudden she felt very weak and foolish.

"Thank you, Miss Meriwether, but there is no need. I can manage the distance from here to my desk."

Trudy stepped back, feeling as if she'd been burned by a fallen moonbeam. Her heart hammered irregularly in her chest.

Matthew carefully took the steps between his chair and the desk, where he sat and opened a drawer. To her dismay he extracted a book of drafts and took up his pen.

"Sir Matthew?"

"I am writing you a draft on my bank for your society."

"But—" This was not how her plan was supposed to work. "Wouldn't you rather see the almshouse for yourself? How do you know I am not a fortune hunter?"

"I did not promise you a fortune, Miss Meriwether. Only a subscription."

"But—" As he handed her a slip of paper, Trudy tried to think of some other enticement, but she couldn't think fast enough. She looked at the signed draft for a generous twenty-five pounds. "I might be a thief all the same. You cannot know if you don't come to visit the almshouse."

"You do not look much like a thief to me," Matthew said with a slight grin. "Although"—his smile faded—"I cannot say that I am a perfect judge of character. Far from it. However, it is easier this way. I shall never know, shall I, if you have cheated me or not. This way I can go blissfully on my way, entirely ignorant of your design.

"Now"—he rose to his feet again, seemingly finished with her—"if you will excuse me, Miss Meriwether, I shall ask Ahmad to escort you home. How did you come here? In a private carriage?"

"No, I—" Flustered by her failure, Trudy was about to say she had floated on the air, but she caught herself in time. "I walked."

"Then Ahmad will be honored to make sure you arrive home without incident."

"No! That is, I would be very grateful, of course, were I not en route to another call. I shall be perfectly all right without his assistance."

Matthew's pupils contracted at her obvious confusion, but though his gaze fell to the draft in her hand, he did not challenge her.

"As you wish," he said in a lifeless tone, which for some reason tore at her heart.

"I wish you would come to see our work, Sir

Matthew. It would do you good, perhaps, to see the ways in which your generous donation will ease the sufferings of these unhappy men."

Matthew declined, and in a tone so firm that she knew she must not press him. But Trudy knew as well that if she could only make him focus on the troubles of others, he would forget his own. That technique had always worked for her. Whenever she had felt her old restlessness growing so strong as to be painful, she had concentrated on somebody else's misery, and the mysterious emptiness within her chest had been filled for a while.

And she had not fabricated her society. She had merely searched until she had found one that was likely to appeal to Matthew, so that he would come outside and follow her into the mists. The only part she had lied about was her own involvement with the group.

But it wouldn't be a lie any longer. She had his draft in her hands, and there was nothing to do but deliver it. And once she had done that, she would instantly become a most valued member of the society.

The thought depressed her. As Ahmad escorted her from the house, his wary eyes never leaving hers for a moment, she wondered what she must do next. Matthew's gift was a good thing, she supposed, but getting it was not the reason she had risked being caught by humans. She had intended to draw Matthew out, out of himself as well as out of doors. Instead, she feared she had merely added to his misery, though she did not know why he seemed so mistrustful of his own kind. Or why he should rather be cheated and stay in ignorance than allow himself to follow her.

If I had known for one minute what Trudy was meanin' to do, I would have stopped her meself. And so I told her when I caught her leaving Sir Matthew's house. Ye could have knocked me down with a feather, ye could, to see her all decked out in them human clothes and walking beside that great beast of a man. He wanted to pop her in a cage, he did; ye could see it in his eyes. He didn't trust her for a minute. No, he did not.

And I was purely that angry that she had gone to see Sir Matthew when he was all right and tight in his head and not delirious with the fever the way I'd always seen him. And in plain daylight, too.

O' course, she insisted that he never suspected she was an elf, so I give 'er that. And I was so relieved to see that she hadn't donned any real human clothes that I forgive 'er. 'Cause that is dangerous to a fairy or an elf. Once they put on human clothes, why, they might just as well be human for all that they can do. 'Cause they lose their powers, ye see, for all the while they've got them wicked garments on.

So I had to be relieved that our Trudy hadn't done anything so harebrained; though, as stubborn as she is, I should have known she wouldn't give up with just one try.

"So," Francis said, once his anger had subsided. "Sir Matthew turned ye down to yer face."

To Trudy he seemed disproportionately pleased that her charm had failed. She frowned. "And what's so good about that? I thought ye wanted me to cheer him up."

"Aye, but I never said nothing about doing it in the daytime when he had all his reason, so it's just as well he's proved too hard for you to trick."

"He's not so hard," Trudy said, with a lift of her chin. "He just knows he's much too weak to go traipsing all over London. Whereas if I make him feel better, I'm sure he'd follow me anywhere."

"Ho! Ho! Got yer dander up, have we?" Francis nearly tumbled over himself with laughter. "And I thought me sister, Trudy, didn't give a fig about her charms. 'Tisn't often that yer beauty fails ye, is it, sister?"

"It didn't fail me. If I had wanted Sir Matthew to follow me, he would have, and make no mistake about it," Trudy said, unable to resist a boast. "But the truth is you don't understand what I was trying to do. The concept of charity is way beyond ye."

Francis's giggle floated out into the air and echoed in the starlight. And he refused to stop his teasing. Nothing would have given Trudy more pleasure in that moment than to tell him she had another plan, but afraid that Francis would try to stop her, she bit her tongue and did not mention it.

He was her brother, a slightly overbearing brother, and he would learn soon enough.

And so I should've watched her, as I told her I would, but ye see, we elves ain't a particularly consistent lot. And so I let meself be distracted from our family business, which I shouldn't have. But I did.

Chapter Three

*M*atthew lay shivering beneath his sheets, the weighted curtains of his bed half drawn against the draft. For many hours since Ahmad's departure, between the periods of intense heat and the longer, more painful bouts of teeth-chattering chill, he had strained to keep his vision lucid. But minutes ago it had started to dim. The ecru plaster of the wall he faced had changed shapes, then come alive. Its wooden frame became a window onto a moving canvas of vicious beasts, both human and brute. A terrifying landscape shifted from desert to jungle and back again, creating shadows of menace to cloud Matthew's mind.

A parade of characters he'd encountered on his explorations passed before his vision: the Ras of Abyssinia, his patrician face endowed with a pair of murderous eyes; the tiny chief of Galla, dipped in butter and riding on a cow; the king of Karagwe, wreathed in smiles as he lay with his fat, milk-fed wives.

And then the panic seized him, clawing with despair: the gut-wrenching knowledge that he might never again see his home, the fear that Helen would never hear a whisper of what had become of him.

He thought of the months he had journeyed, the endless months he had been held captive, unable by trick or strategem to send her any kind of message. Would she wait and wait for word until she, too, was dead?

He pictured her sitting by the fire, unaware of his hard-won success. The fame and glory he had sought burned to mere ashes and air. And his discoveries, for which he'd sacrificed so much, what were they but deserts and lakes and swamps drawn in cruelty and pain?

He was weak—too weak to mount a vigorous escape, too weak even to mount a horse. And Ahmad carried him mile after mile through black-mired ground to their freedom.

He fought to stay alive, fought to keep Helen's face before him like an altar piece.

And then her face was floating near his eyes. A woman's face, pale with worry. Faye.

"Are ye all right, mannie?" she said, with a frown.

"Faye? M-Miss Meriwether?" He struggled to sit, but she pressed his feverish body down with one cool hand on his forehead. Matthew collapsed against his pillow. She had found him out. She had discovered all those times this past week her image had entered his mind, even though he had ruthlessly banished all frivolous thought of her from his head. He had even fought the temptation to use her image to hold his nightmares at bay.

She had discovered his secret, but what was she doing in his bedroom?

When he would have asked, attempting with a scowl to gather his dignity about him, she stopped his lips with her fingertips.

"It's not Faye," she said soothingly.

But it was. She had the same meadow green eyes, the same short, black hair, so brilliant it shone like diamonds, the same impish mouth. The only things he saw that confused him were a set of pointed ears he did not recall her having and a change of clothes. Her elegant dress with its silken sheen had been changed for a simple tunic of green felt.

Matthew closed his eyes and knew at once that he was hallucinating again.

"No, you're not Faye," he said, shaking with fatigue, "but you're a welcome sight for all that."

"Do ye know who I am then, mannie?"

"An elf maid sent to tempt me, I suppose."

"That's right. Me brother Francis said he told ye all about me."

Matthew gave a deep laugh. It surprised him, coming so close upon his nightmare, the memory of which made his laughter fade.

He opened his eyes, wondering if she had gone, but found her just where he had left her, hovering over his face. With her curious stare she looked so real, he could almost reach out and touch her cheek, which seemed as pink and soft as a rose petal.

But when he raised his hand to try, she vanished. Distraught, he fought to sit and saw her perched upon the footboard of his bed.

"Can't let ye do that, mannie." She sounded breathless. "I promised me brother I wouldn't let ye catch me."

"I wasn't trying to catch you. I was simply seeing if you were real. Which is patently insane," he muttered, falling back against the pillows again.

Insane as it was, he still desired her company. Beautiful visions were far more welcome than his wilder hallucinations, no matter how firmly he'd put her from his mind. It did no good for a man in his condition to delude himself consciously with thoughts of a lady he would never see again. Especially one so young and charming. What would she see in him except a man broken in health whose life had ended at the ripe old age of twenty-seven? No, that way lay heartache.

But since this was a dream or a hallucination or mere illusion, he might as well give up and enjoy it.

"What was your name again? Hortense? Or Hermione, or some such?"

Her lips drew into the loveliest pout he had ever seen. "The name is Trudy if ye don't mind."

Matthew never had cared for ladies' pouts, seeing them as mere artifice designed to make men want to kiss them, but he did like Trudy's. Urges he had thought buried along with his engagement to Helen stirred in him again.

"I beg your pardon," he said, restraining a smile. It was strange how a dream could make him want to smile when nothing else had for so long. "Now, would you care to entertain me with the story of how you came into my bedroom? Something along the lines of the whopper you told before?"

She gazed at him warily. "I thought I told ye I wasn't her."

"And so you did. But you are she, nonetheless. My imagined vision of Miss Meriwether."

"Are ye so sure then?" A sly smile graced her lips.

"Quite sure."

"And why would ye be imagining about her?"

Surprised at himself, Matthew felt a flush stealing through his body, as if he were a mere callow youth caught in a display of cream-pot love.

Since this was a dream, however, he could afford to be honest. "Because she's the loveliest thing I've seen in some time."

Trudy's brows shot up. "Truly? Ye didn't act as if ye thought so." The resentment on her face made him grin. Then she muttered something that confused him: "By all rights, she should be the most beautiful sight ye've *ever* seen."

"Why?"

"Herumph!" Trudy crossed her arms in a gesture of pique that reminded him strongly of Francis, only Matthew realized at once that indeed she was more ravishing than anything he'd ever imagined before. Even in his delusion, however, he could not bring himself to say such a thing aloud.

With his head propped on the pillows, he could just see her delicate body and her enchanting face between the tall posts of his bed. The curtains fell on either side of her, making a stage, as if she were putting on a private performance for his sake.

The ache of ague racked his joints, and he ought to want nothing so much as the oblivion of sleep. Still, he kept his eyes open for the pleasure of watching her. When he'd closed them, he had found that her image faded quickly, just as Francis's did, whereas his other dreams always seemed to be enhanced.

"So." She seemed strangely ill at ease for an illusion. "Ye did find her passable at least."

"Far more than that."

"Then why did ye let her go without asking to see her again?"

He shook his head and sighed. "My dear girl, I quite see you are taking the part of devil's advocate, but there is no point, truly."

"Why?"

"Because I shall never tilt at windmills again."

"And why would it be tilting at windmills to see what she did with yer money?"

Because I would not be going to see where my money was spent so much as to see her again, which was what you asked.

Strange, Matthew felt suddenly, but this conversation had none of the logic his speech with Francis always did. It was more like the twisted talk ladies engaged in when they were hoping for compliments. He would not be manipulated by his own delusion, though he could enjoy the way her pixielike features betrayed her every emotion from hope to joy to chagrin.

He discovered a perverse wish inside himself to make her smile.

"I should not see Miss Meriwether again for fear of making a fool of myself."

To his intense delight, a blush suffused her face. "Yer never a fool."

"Oh no?" The memory of his most foolish moment slapped him in the face. "I beg to differ. It is certainly most foolish to nourish feelings for a faithless woman."

"Sure and it is. But ye don't know, do ye, if Faye is such a one."

"I was not speaking of Faye."

Trudy felt the bitterness in his words like a weight down deep inside her stomach. So he had been lured by someone before, and to no end. That was why he had not wished to follow her.

She stared at Matthew's ravaged face, shadowed by the bed curtains, and could almost feel the intense heat emanating from his body. Some would be due to the fever, of course, but that last almost-blast had come from the fury inside him. She knew he was angry with himself, however, and not with the woman who'd abused him.

A desire to make him forget all about that woman grew powerfully inside her.

She tried another tack. "If ye feel that way, then there's nothing to worry about. Ye'll never have to see this Faye again. But it seems ye've forgotten about one thing, at least."

She liked the way his dark eyes glowed darker when he responded to her.

"What would that one thing be?"

"That it's the Yuletide, the time to be generous to yer inferiors. Don't ye think ye should be thinking of others and not of yerself?"

He raised an offended eyebrow. "Am I mistaken? Did I not just give that young lady a draft for twenty-five pounds?"

"Sure and ye did. But there are others who are

needful, ye know, and it might do ye some good to think of their misery instead of yer own."

"Now you even sound like Miss Faye Meriwether." The similarity did not seem to disgust him, though. As he focused his feverish eyes on her, a slight grin tipped the corner of his mouth.

Trudy gathered courage from his expression. "Then ye ought, at least, to go see that yer money's been put to good use. Can ye even be sure that she did with it what she should?"

Matthew smiled and his gaze drifted, as if she were nothing more than his own voice in his ear. Trudy wanted to pinch him to show him how real she was, but she was afraid to get that close. She had seen the strength in his arms beneath his bedclothes and had no doubt he could trap her if he desired.

"Well?"

Matthew brought his piercing gaze back to hers. "I have a feeling that Miss Meriwether is indeed the person she pretends to be. There was something quite genuine about her."

"Oh? You think so?" Trudy asked, holding her breath, surprised by how much his opinion mattered. She was immensely flattered that her trick had been so well received.

But then she had felt almost human. In his library, concerned for his welfare and wishing nothing more than that he would follow her, she had had all the doubts and fears that poor humans were subject to. If he had believed her, then her emotions must have added some truth to her performance.

"Yes." He answered her question, and fatigue seemed to sweep relentlessly over him. His voice faltered. "I do believe she was genuine, so there is no cause for me to find her."

"But don't ye want to? Aren't ye tired of being here inside this house, sitting in yer chair?"

"Yes, I'm tired. But I am ill, too, and I shall not embarrass myself by falling down on my face in the street."

"Oh, is that all it is?" Trudy felt relief. "Well, I can help ye with that."

Matthew closed his eyes, and a derisive smile twisted his lips. "Delusion upon delusion," he murmured.

"Not at all." Trudy drew herself up.

She could help him. She knew she could, given time. It was not in her power to cure him with one simple tap of a fairy wand or a miraculous potion, but her magic was powerful nonetheless. If he would simply trust her enough to relax with her, then her voice alone would bring him some relief from his aches and pains. And if she could ever get him to promise that he would not try to capture her, her touch could do much more.

She stood and tiptoed like a leaf in the wind closer to his head, not even leaving a dent in the coverlets. "Just keep yer eyes closed, mannie, while I talk to you," she said soothingly, and saw him acquiesce. The muscles in his face seemed to relax.

"You have a musical voice," he murmured.

"Aye. I'm glad ye like it," she said. "It'll do ye some good."

She could feel the pain easing out of his shoulders as she talked.

"Just relax, mannie," she crooned. "Relax and

think about me, or this Faye if ye want. No harm in a little thought."

Another grin made his brows arch like a wolf's. "You think not?" he said. "Then your thoughts must be more innocent than mine."

A rush of blood started in her toes and ended in her face, nearly making her choke.

"Ye think what ye like, mannie; just don't tell me any of the details, mind?"

"Never fear." A deep, rumbling chuckle stirred his chest, but Matthew kept his eyes closed.

Which was a very good thing, Trudy decided, for her curiosity had brought her dangerously near his face again. She could reach out and touch his lips if she wanted, or run her fingers through his hair.

And it was not at all curious that she should want to do these things, for she knew they were designed to give pleasure both ways, and countless elves had pleased themselves with humans thus. The danger lay in giving in to this urge before the man could be lured into elfland. Once there, it would be he, and not she, who was trapped.

"Let me sing to you, mannie," she whispered, "until you fall asleep."

The next morning Matthew was surprised by how well he felt. Sometime during the night his fever had passed away without leaving him in its usual lake of perspiration, and it had not wrung him out as on all former such occasions. The bout had lasted a much shorter time, too. Mere hours instead of long days. For the first time in more than a year, he had hope that its ravagements would someday abate.

He dressed fully and made his way down the stairs. Ahmad served his breakfast, content to act the manservant for want of other employment. As grateful as he was for this man's friendship, Matthew found himself wishing for an English servant this morning. His appetite, long missing, had returned with a vengeance, and he would have relished a large plate of bacon. Ahmad naturally could not be requested to overlook his religious objections to pork.

"The saab is better this morning." The Pathan's dark gaze looked him over approvingly.

"Yes, I am."

"Did you dream the dreams of the holy?"

A smirk tugged at Matthew's scarred lip. "I'm afraid Miss Meriwether would not have said so."

Never obtuse, Ahmad raised his thick brows, and his eyes sparkled. "If such is the case, Matthew saab, then you must indeed be well."

"Not completely cured, but well enough that I have given some thought to a morning outing."

His announcement brought an unmistakable look of delight to Ahmad's face, such a great delight that Matthew suffered a pang of remorse. In his illness and bitter disappointment, he had not considered how his friend might feel, cooped up in a London house with a man not fit even to make good company. Yet Ahmad had tended him without complaint these many months with no diversions. This realization determined Matthew to go out much more than his faint new restlessness for activity for himself. And it overcame the niggling fear that he had proposed such an outing in the hope of seeing Miss Meriwether again.

Trudy's reminder last night that it was the Yuletide had done nothing to inspire him to charitable deeds. But Ahmad's needs were altogether a different matter. Matthew remembered it was the custom at Christmas to turn all relationships topsy-turvy. At his school, the boys had become masters, serving none but the Lord of Misrule, who had been elected from among them and directed their games. In some households, the owners served their servants on Christmas Eve.

Matthew decided that in the spirit of the Yule he should turn the tables on his friend, at least enough to provide him with some exercise.

"We shall hire a carriage," he said. "Where would you like to go?"

Ahmad opened his mouth to speak before confusion bathed his features. "I do not know, saab. I am still a stranger in your land."

Once again Matthew felt the sting of shame. "Well, it is time you saw something of it besides the market at Covent Garden." He searched his mind for some diversion that would interest his companion without offending his Mohammedan sensibilities. In truth, when he had first thought of going out, Trudy's admonition that he should visit the almshouse had seemed the logical choice. Without any better aim, such a visit would have satisfied his need for a destination, but now, with Ahmad's needs foremost . . .

All at once, the suitability of his intended outing struck him. What Ahmad undoubtedly missed most were people of his own kind. Even though he was an Afghan by birth, his travels had taken him all over the Mohammedan lands. He was fluent in both Arabic and Ki-Swahili, and legend claimed his people to be of Persian descent. Surely in this almshouse of Africans he would find men of his own religion at least.

"I have just the place in mind," Matthew said. "Now all we have to do is find it."

He finished his meal, trying to remember whether Faye had given him the address of the almshouse, but no such memory came to him. As he rose from the table, he wondered how difficult it would be to track it down. No matter how much better he felt this morning, he knew his strength would not last through a daylong search.

As he left the small dining room, his eye was caught by the sight of a salver lying on a table in the passageway. A card lay upon it.

Unaware of any other visitors besides Faye in the past few days, Matthew picked it up.

Engraved in elegant gold letters was her name, Miss Faye Meriwether, followed by the words "The Society for the Relief of Indigent African Natives" with an address on Whitfield Street and a notation "South of Tottenham Court Road."

"Ahmad," Matthew said to the man who had just caught up with him, "did Miss Meriwether leave her card with you?"

"No, saab." Ahmad stared at the card in Matthew's hand, and his black brows snapped together. "Where did you find that?"

Matthew gestured at the plate on the table. "It was here."

"No, saab. That card was not on the salver. Neither yesterday, nor this morning before you broke your fast."

"Unless Miss Meriwether can walk through wood, it must have been. I'm afraid your famed eyesight must be deserting you, my friend."

"No, saab!"

"Well, no matter," Matthew said, though a fresh worry had entered his head. Clearly, from the look on Ahmad's face, he had a greater need for rest than he had allowed. It was one thing for Matthew in his state of self-absorption not to have noticed the card earlier, quite another for Ahmad to have missed it. He had twice let a diminutive lady sneak past him. Matthew had no doubt that Faye had left the card unobtrusively on her way out, hoping its discovery would act as a reminder of her call. She clearly wished to spur him to greater efforts to the benefit of her society.

Not wishing to upset his friend, who appeared to be more than a trifle disconcerted about his lapse, Matthew let the subject drop, pledging to himself that he would never again allow his own selfishness to harm Ahmad.

Trudy had, in fact, slipped the card onto the salver while Matthew and Ahmad were eating, having rejoiced over Matthew's change of heart. She had decided that a small reminder might not be taken amiss, and besides, she had no wish to wait all day for Matthew to remember the address of the almshouse.

Now all she had to worry about was how best to contrive an accidental meeting. Not that a simple ruse would be all that difficult, but she had far rather do something exciting. She wondered if she dared conjure a carriage of her own, complete with a dashing team of horses. She pictured herself tooling around London seated on the box of a high-perch phaeton of the sort she had seen in Hyde Park. She recalled one particular lady who had attracted many admirers with hers. Trudy thought she might be able to persuade her cousin Grace and her aunt Petunia to pose as the horses, though assuredly Grace would insist on having a turn to drive herself.

No, it would be far better under the circumstances not to involve any other elves. Trudy would not put it past Grace to take a fancy to Matthew and attempt to lead him into elfland as her own swain. And once she had caught on to Trudy's latest escapade, she might decide it would be fun to pose as a London ingenue, too.

With these sobering reflections in mind, Trudy skipped around to Tottenham Court Road, designing a whole new ensemble to wear on the way.

By the time she spied Matthew and Ahmad stepping down from a hired carriage in Whitfield Street, she had dressed herself in a becoming shade of pale green. A redingote of yellow cloth with velvet trim and padded sleeves covered her gown to her ankles, and a green silk bonnet with a fashionably high crown decked her head. She had copied the outfit from a pattern book she'd found in a store in Bond Street, and she thought it vastly became her.

Sir Matthew must have thought so, too, for when he saw her coming down the street, his eyes lit. His nostrils flared as his gaze swept her from head to toe, and he barely hid a smile. A natural flush of pleasure warmed her as she greeted him on a note of surprise.

"Sir Matthew! What a fortunate meeting, sir. I had not dared to believe you would come around."

"Perhaps not," he said, "but you had a fairly good guess that I might."

Trudy did not pretend to misunderstand him but gave him a coy look. "Let us just say I hoped that the spirit of the season would inspire you."

Now that she had approached him, she offered him her hand, which he took with a bow. She couldn't help admiring the way his jacket stretched across his broad shoulders, though it hung fairly loosely about his waist, revealing the weight he had lost. A cravat was knotted carelessly about his neck, which showed he had no care for fashion. The casual appearance of it suited him far better than the starched knot and high shirt points she had seen on other men.

Aware of his friend, who was observing them with interest, Trudy held out her hand to him. "Good morning, Ahmad."

Taken aback, the Pathan hesitated only a moment before making his salaam. Turning to Matthew, Trudy was surprised to see a warm look upon his face. Then she realized that a real London ingenue would undoubtedly have ignored Ahmad, if she had not gaped at him instead, and she understood the reason for his approbation.

"Shall we go in?" she said with a sweeping gesture at the building behind Matthew.

Matthew offered her his arm, and Trudy slipped her hand inside the crook of his elbow, tremblingly aware of the sturdy muscles beneath his sleeve.

They were admitted through a gate by a stooped, dark-skinned man in floor-length robes, who bowed his respects to them. Trudy greeted him as she would an old friend. This was not her first visit, since she had delivered Matthew's draft on the very day he had presented it to her. She had tried to acquaint herself then with the names of the alms-house staff, but the steward of the facility had been away. She had nothing more from which to recognize him now than his name and a sketchy description.

As they strolled through the narrow courtyard, leading back to the common rooms, a gray-haired gentleman in Quakerish dress issued from a doorway to their left. He looked plainly astonished to see them.

Taking her heart in her hands, Trudy slipped out of Matthew's grasp to greet the stranger with open arms. "Oh, there you are, you dear, dear man!"

Chapter Four

The man, who was surely Mr. Thomas Waite, steward of the establishment, halted in round-eyed astonishment upon hearing Trudy's effusive greeting. She was certain he had never been met quite so enthusiastically in his life, but she had hoped that the rapidity of her assault combined with her dazzling beauty would stop his tongue from giving her away.

Still, as his look of shock turned to fear that the unknown creature bearing down on him seemed intent upon an embrace, she thought better of it and scooped his hand into both of hers instead.

"Dear Mr. Waite, I have brought a visitor to see you, the same generous benefactor who recently became one of our number. May I present Sir Matthew Dunstone?"

As she had hoped, Matthew's name, being the one on the large draft Mr. Waite had just received, distracted the poor steward for the moment. His eyes lit and he pounced on Matthew, wringing his hand.

"Yes, indeed. Good day to you, sir. You honor us most profoundly with your visit."

Matthew, whose jaw had tensed inexplicably

when his name had been mentioned, relaxed at this simple greeting, but Trudy could see he had no interest in being thanked.

"Not at all," he said with a look of polite boredom. "I have only come as the result of a mild case of curiosity and with the thought that my companion Ahmad, who has traveled widely in Africa, might find something to interest him in your work."

As Mr. Waite turned curiously to examine the immense Pathan at Matthew's side, Matthew directed his gaze toward Trudy, and his expression eased.

"However," he added with a challenging glint in his eye, "I should say that you could have sent no more determined ambassador for your cause than Miss Meriwether here."

"Miss Meriwether?" A dazed, befuddled look came over their host before he fixed his gaze on her.

Trudy cursed herself for letting Matthew's smile distract her from the need to keep her deception working. If she did not hurry, the reason for Mr. Waite's confusion would be eminently clear. She should have known that neither his joy nor his surprise on meeting his mysterious benefactor could long prevent him from asking who the devil she was.

Rallying quickly, she threw Mr. Waite an arch glance full of intimacy. "Sir, I must protest this formality! Why, when two hearts beat nearly as one for a cause as noble as ours, the conventions should never apply. From this day forward, I beg you will call me Faye."

As she had hoped, her boldness made him gape

with a wide open jaw, and his accompanying silence lasted long enough for her to slip in another diversion. "We should not keep Sir Matthew standing any longer than is absolutely necessary, however, for he has been extremely ill and I fear this exertion may tire him. May we not," she continued, "see if these gentlemen would like to tour the establishment? I suspect that is why they have come."

No host when faced with a request on behalf of a generous patron can pursue another course. Startled into performing his duties, Mr. Waite became instant cordiality.

"Of course, of course!" With an anxious glance, the steward at once took in Matthew's sallow tinge and the looseness of his clothing. "We shall start at once."

Trudy could hardly blame Mr. Waite for not remarking these telltale signs of Matthew's illness sooner, for the deep intelligence of his eyes, the immense force of character shining through them, nearly made her ignore the results of his ague as well. If her own thoughts had not been so focused on distracting him with the hope of vanquishing his vicious dreams, she might not remark them at all. As it was, she could barely keep herself from hovering over him, from offering him her arm, or from reaching up to touch his forehead to see if his fever had returned.

It would be ridiculous to act like a hen over her chick, and yet something about Matthew made Trudy feel quite protective of him. Possessive, too, like a gleeful troll with his hoard of gold.

The almshouse was laid out in a long, narrow

rectangle around the courtyard in which they stood. In his eagerness to engage Matthew's further interest, Mr. Waite started to lead them along the walk to its end.

"If you will, please, come this way . . ."

Matthew offered Trudy his arm again, which she accepted with an unbidden rush of warmth. He was so tall, her chin barely reached the top button of his vest. The brush of his sleeve against her hair made her feel strangely shy, when she had not felt so last night in circumstances far more compromising. Perhaps it was because he looked more intently at her now, as if she were an intriguing sprite, more real than she had been at night, when the reverse was true.

As much as she found she enjoyed being the object of his scrutiny, Trudy was relieved when Matthew politely turned his attention to their host.

"As you can see," Mr. Waite was saying, "these are the dormitories. Each resident occupies his own room. We have twenty-two inmates, all of them male and somewhat incapacitated by age. In general they were brought to England to act as servants. Then, for whatever reason, most were left to fend for themselves, although some are living here as pensioners of the same families who brought them to this country."

"What is their occupation now?" Matthew asked, and Trudy took hope from the interest in his voice.

Mr. Waite said, "We have taught them to make yarn and to weave, which, as it appears, is done by the men in most of their countries. We thought it best to find an occupation which would not offend their religious sensibilities."

"Very wise." Matthew's wry comment seemed to suggest that he had witnessed what sometimes happened when the opposite attempt was made.

At that moment they reached the end of the walk, and Mr. Waite led them inside the small common rooms, which stood in place of the usual chapel. In each a group of men sat occupied in various tasks having to do with a stage of preparing wool. Some were carding, some dyeing and spinning, some weaving. Trudy felt her own curiosity growing. However, mindful that she must appear as if these sights were familiar to her, she cast no curious glances their way.

At the sight of a group of men in long, white robes, Ahmad, who had been following them at a discreet distance, chose to stop. The men glanced up from their work.

An exchange of words transpired in Arabic. Trudy, to whom all tongues were known, recognized the greetings as cordial.

Turning back to his own party, Ahmad fixed his stare on Matthew. Trudy supposed he was examining his friend for signs of fatigue.

"Saab," he said, apparently satisfied. "If you would not be inconvenienced, I should like to converse with these men."

"Not at all. You must do as you wish. If I tire, I can easily wait for you in the carriage."

Ahmad bowed and entered the room where the men were working.

"You yourself have traveled widely, Sir Matthew?" Mr. Waite's inquiry made them turn their heads.

Trudy could feel a bunching of the muscles in Matthew's arm. "Yes."

"Then you are perhaps familiar with the Mohammedan tongue?"

Matthew gave a curt nod, and Trudy could tell he had no wish to be questioned further. His tightly compressed lips barely concealed his impatience.

A nervous flutter of Mr. Waite's eyelids showed he had sensed Matthew's reserve. "Forgive my curiosity, sir. I had merely hoped you would be willing to help me with a particular inmate who seems to have landed here with no knowledge whatsoever of English. Though his fellows are quite willing to act as his interpreter, none are fluent enough to make his trouble clear to me."

"If that is all you require"—Matthew again relaxed—"then Ahmad should be able to assist you. When it comes to African tongues, he is far more gifted than I."

He called Ahmad back out of the room, and they conferred to one side. Afraid that Mr. Waite would use the opportunity to try to establish who she was, Trudy kept him occupied with various questions of her own. She could not hear the other men's conversation, but bits and pieces of it floated to her ears. Matthew clearly wanted Ahmad to stay at the almshouse as long as he wished, while Ahmad was concerned by the thought of Matthew's going home alone.

At last Matthew's strength of character carried the day, assisted by a glare from his powerful eyes.

While many other men would have quaked beneath it, Ahmad merely conceded defeat with a deep salaam.

Matthew rejoined Trudy and their host and gave Mr. Waite to know that Ahmad would stay to render him whatever service was needed but that he himself must retire.

"I have errands of my own to complete also," Trudy said quickly, not wanting to be trapped with Mr. Waite and his questions. "I shall accompany you to the door."

Mr. Waite thanked them both for coming and begged they would do so again. At least, Trudy thought, as she and Matthew approached the court-yard, the steward of the almshouse was no longer staring at her as if she'd fallen from the sky. No doubt he had put his confusion behind him, merely grateful to have two new interested patrons for his house.

As they came out, Trudy said, "I hope this morning has not tired you excessively."

"Not at all. You quite mistake my actions."

She had offended him once again with her solicitude. Matthew, it seemed, did not care for sympathy, far less for anyone's pity, but she could not help being concerned for his health. Fortunately, as she examined him covertly, he showed no particular signs of fatigue. Instead, a hint of restlessness flickered in his eyes.

She arched a look, at once feeling conspiratorial. "Very well, sir, what was your design in escaping? Did you find Mr. Waite uninspiring?"

"No. Though at one time I would have despised a

man such as he, who did nothing more than a pedestrian job day after day. But that is a young man's opinion, and I have learned there is something to be said for devotion of any kind.

"No," he continued, not giving her time to respond to his curious statement. "I simply wanted to give Ahmad a bit of time to himself. He has been spending far too much of it alone with me."

"I see. And shall you return home as you said?"

Matthew's deep brown eyes lit with a glimmer. His tall brow furrowed as he hesitated, as if torn between two very different options. "I had thought I might take a turn in the park," he said with his gaze fixed on her. "May I take you up?"

Trudy sighed, and a beam of pleasure bathed her lips in warmth. "I cannot think of anything more delightful than a carriage ride just now."

She had startled him with her boldness, but it intrigued him nonetheless. Eyeing her with a mixture of wariness and amusement, he said nothing more but ushered her out of the courtyard and into his waiting vehicle.

Matthew had hired a closed chaise. Trudy knew it was most improper for her to ride inside it with a gentleman alone, but she also knew deeply that Matthew would care even less for the rules of propriety than she. Why would a man who had roamed such exotic parts of the world have the same ridiculous standards as other Englishmen?

Matthew sat facing the rear, giving her the forward-facing seat. He settled a lap rug over her knees and directed the driver to take them to the park. Trudy heard the crack of his whip and felt the carriage give a short lunge before the horses settled into a sedate pace.

Clasping the seat with both hands and swinging her feet, for they did not reach the floor, she watched delightedly as the scenery rolled past. This was her first ride in a human conveyance, and she had rather hoped there would be more dash. But she found she was not disappointed, for the illicit pleasure of being alone with Matthew more than made up for the demure ride.

The storefronts they saw were decked with freshly cut greens, a sure sign the Yule was upon them. And when they passed an elegant milliner's shop, she exclaimed over the hats in its bow window. But instead of peering outside as she did, Matthew kept his gaze fixed on her, an analytical smile curving his lips.

Trudy tried to engage him in the sights they were passing. The brisk temperature of early winter never failed to arouse her excitement since it hailed the coming year. The air in the carriage was nippy enough to chill her nose.

"You are quite a mystery, Miss Meriwether." Matthew's voice cut across her effusions about the high-perch phaeton they had just passed.

"Faye. Please," she said, hoping to divert him from the questions she feared were gathering.

"Don't you wish to know what I find so mysterious about you—Faye?"

"Of course." When her ruse failed, a nervous feeling rose in her stomach like bubbles blown by a nymph in a pond. "What woman would not wish to know the answer to a riddle such as that?"

"What woman indeed? But you are not like other women, are you?"

She tensed with the fear of discovery. "What on earth can you mean?"

"You are more than simply unconventional. You hardly seem aware of the restraints upon women of your class."

Trudy breathed as relief soothed the flutterings inside her. "I am fully aware of them, Sir Matthew, but I despise them. You have traveled, sir. You know that the restraints imposed upon women differ widely from culture to culture."

"Yes." His brow furrowed. "But how would you know?"

"Oh." She waved an airy hand. "I have been about the world a bit, too. My father was a traveler, like you."

"Let me guess. The army in India, followed by a stint in the diplomatic service?"

She smiled, pleased that she did not have to invent another lie. Matthew had done the work for her. "Precisely," she said, and then was dismayed by how bad even that small inverse lie made her feel, when she was so used to inventing tales. She sensed that Matthew would be hurt if he knew she had lied. And she found she did not wish to hurt him.

Feeling guilty for perhaps the first time in her life, Trudy saw that Matthew's eyes had narrowed, as if the evidence of her crime could be read on her face. She recovered and treated him to her most bewitching glance and was relieved to see him blink.

Pulling his gaze from her as if by force, Matthew

shifted awkwardly on his bench, and Trudy dared to hope that a fleeting thought of ravishment had crossed his mind. Francis had been right when he'd said that Matthew would be a tough nut to crack. Any other man would have done his best to capture her after one of her saucy glances.

"Are you sure you are quite comfortable?" she probed, perversely determined to get confirmation of her hopes.

A grin quirked his mouth, but "Quite" was all he said.

"Tell me," he added, once they had gone a few more blocks and his mood had become pensive. "Why do I get the feeling that Mr. Waite scarcely knows you?"

Trudy's heart dived into her stomach again. The vexing man! Did he notice everything? With a genuine sigh, she tried to explain his suspicions away.

"Mr. Waite is a worthy individual in many ways, but I fear my freethinking manner shocks him. Perhaps you noticed that he almost seemed afraid of me. I fear my independence is quite beyond his experience of females."

"As it is of mine. Not that I censure you for it. But I cannot help wondering how it came about."

"Oh, that is quite easy." Her words, when she produced them, had more than a hint of truth. "My parents both died very young." *For elves*. Though both would have been considered ancient by human standards.

"And have you no brothers or sisters?"

Trudy hesitated, but this telling the truth was

addicting. "I have one brother, but we do not live together."

Seeing that some elaboration was needed, she continued, "My brother prefers the country. He is not fond of human company, whereas I—"

"Whereas you devote yourself to worthy causes?"

"Yes."

"Which presupposes that you control your own fortune."

She paused over the mot juste. "Let us simply say that I have resources under my own governance and may do as I please with them."

"What does your brother have to say about these activities—calling on strange men, walking the streets without an escort?"

Trudy gave an impish shrug, accompanied by a laugh. "I fear he knows very little about them, though he would undoubtedly disapprove. He's very stuffy."

"Stranger and stranger still. And have you no thought to your own danger?"

"No." Trudy drew herself up and folded her hands in her lap with a smile of the purest satisfaction. "I am entirely fearless."

Matthew's brows arched, and he slowly pulled back in his seat as if he did not quite know what to make of such a remark. Trudy feared that she might have given him reason for disgust. She had been carried away by the freedom that comes from telling the truth, but truth was a sticky business, one she had better have more care to.

"Have I shocked you, Sir Matthew?" Anxiety tightened around her heart. They had made two rounds of the park now, and she feared their ride would soon be over, and she wondered whether he would ever want to see her again. She could always appear to him at night and try to engineer his desires, but she had far rather the idea come from him.

"No." He relaxed his challenged posture. "I simply have never met a woman quite like you, with the exception, perhaps, of one African princess, the wife of a vizier."

"Was she beautiful?" Trudy didn't know where the question had come from.

"Yes. Very beautiful. And intelligent, too, which is much more important. She saved my life more than once with her advice and intervention."

"Did you love her?"

"Completely, but not in the way you are asking. My feelings were greatly tinged by respect and a healthy dose of fear for the power she wielded."

"Oh." Trudy sighed, inexplicably relieved. "Then what you felt, Sir Matthew, was not love. It was awe."

A glint of respect lit his eyes. "You understand the situation perfectly, which in itself is curious. How a lady of your age, who acts for all the world as if she's never ridden in a carriage before, can be so wise is more than a bit mysterious."

"I wasn't acting as if I'd never been in a carriage before—was I?"

Matthew felt a laugh burst from him. Her indignation, followed so closely by doubt, enchanted him. "Forgive me," he said with exaggerated politeness. "I must have been gravely mistaken."

But the smile that had visited his lips lingered in his chest. It felt strange after so many months of bitterness, but he could almost feel the strength of his amusement in his blood. Never before had he met a female with so many contradictions, all delightful.

Faye was daintily built and as fresh of face as a wood nymph, yet she showed the same confidence in her cause as a battle-hardened general. She could not be more feminine or graceful, yet she acted with the sweeping freedom of a man. If she had one fault, it would appear to be conceit, for he'd often heard a certain smugness in her tone. Yet her version of conceit had none of the viciousness displayed by petty women. It seemed so much a part of her, he could not even fault her for a weakness he usually despised.

But—Matthew felt the pain from old wounds urging him to caution—he did not really know her or know who she was. She'd appeared on his doorstep without so much as a letter of introduction and had gained entry with the use of artifice. Even today there had been times when he had sensed she was not being truthful. She plainly would have preferred to evade his questions, and her nervous glances had given her away more surely than her otherwise polished answers.

Her entire appearance and her performance were so perfect, in fact, as to seem ephemeral. Where her charm and her rare beauty might have tempted him to pursue her, were he a healthy man with glowing prospects, there was something about her very perfection that gave him pause. Strangely it was those very moments of doubt and unease that had made her more real and all the more appealing.

He did not want to expose himself to a woman without principle again. Faye might still be a fortune hunter. He was not a wealthy man, but his modest estate was enough to maintain him in a certain comfort for the rest of his life. He was not such a fool that he did not perceive how attractive such a life would be to a woman who needed it.

He shook himself from these dangerous musings, asking abruptly, "Why did you call on me, Faye?"

She looked startled. "I have already told you, and now shown you, that our charity was in need—"

"No, you misunderstood me. I was asking, why me?"

Her eyes widened. Where once he had thought them green, they now appeared a deep, brooding violet. But after he pressed his eyes closed and felt fatigue sweeping suddenly through him, he discovered they were green again. His fever must be returning.

Fighting to keep this knowledge from her, ashamed to be betrayed by his own weakness, he sat as still as possible. But a softening of her face told him she had noticed that all was not well.

"I had hoped," she began, "to persuade you to approach your friends on behalf of my society."

"Friends?" Matthew knew that harshness had sprung into his voice. "Whomever can you mean?"

Faye blinked. "The African Association? Are they not the group that sent you on your expedition? I had hoped they would take a particular interest in our almshouse."

Matthew fought the gripping fury that name always evoked, leaving shakiness in its wake. At once he knew he had overtaxed his ravaged body today.

"I am afraid," he said with a terrible stillness, "you have been grossly deceived. I have lost whatever influence I once wielded with that group."

Faye's eyes grew round with dismay. He could almost see her cringing from the despair on his face. Matthew averted his glance, pinching his brow to spare her the sight.

"Surely that cannot be true," she ventured after an interminable pause.

"I'm quite afraid that it is. But it's a long story, one I will not bore you with."

Concern and restrained curiosity played across her face, but he would not give in to them. He had already revealed too much. Let her hear from others how seriously he had been discredited, he thought.

Then, all at once, a radical change came over her demeanor. A militant gleam lit her eyes.

"If you have lost your former friends," she said with a mischievous dimple in each cheek, "that is all the more reason to introduce them to me."

"What?" Matthew gave an incredulous bark of laughter.

"I said, it would be better to let me speak to them."

"Oh?" He studied her. Something in her look made him wish to hear more. "To say what precisely?"

"Oh"—that smug little chin of hers was in the air again—"nothing in particular. But," she added with a wink, "I assure you I have my ways of dealing with foolish men."

Sir Joseph Banks, a fool? Some of the profoundest minds of their day, mere foolish men? Matthew wanted to break into laughter. But, he realized with a start, any such outburst from him would be of pure exhilaration, untinged by spite. When he puzzled over his reaction, the explanation immediately came: Faye believed in him.

She had not asked what he had done to lose the respect of such an august body. She gave no sign of believing his ostracism was merited. Without a blink or a justification from him, she had taken his side.

Such blind acceptance had given him the greatest lift he'd had since he'd begun to believe he would make it home alive from his last expedition. And that former rush had lasted so brief a time. Just long enough for him to return home to find his reputation ruined and his fiancée married to someone else.

The immensity of that disappointment, the dashing of his fondest dreams, should have made him cautious now, but he found that despite the extreme exhaustion that threatened to overtake him, he did not want to give up this one spark of hope. It might be mad in the extreme—it most assuredly was—but something inside him very much wanted to see what Faye would accomplish with those men.

They might think him a liar, a coward, and a scoundrel, but at least they would see he had very good taste and the support of one very charming person—which was just what his vanity needed.

They were all gentlemen. There was no possibility that they would treat her with rudeness, especially not with her pretty face.

Glancing at Faye now and feeling the immense pull of her charm, Matthew could almost feel pity for those men. They were extremely competitive. He could practically see them elbowing each other out of the way for a chance to make fools of themselves.

"Very well," he said before fatigue and reason could make him change his mind. "I can take you to their next dinner meeting, which should be this Saturday. But I must warn you, the governing committee meets in a tavern in Pall Mall. Are you certain you wish to appear?"

"Absolutely," she said, and he could not doubt it. "As soon as you determine for certain what time we should go, you must drop me a note at this address." She reached into her reticule for a card and handed it to him.

Like the first, it was engraved in gold. Not the usual fancy of a fortune hunter. Matthew felt absurdly relieved by this proof that she was what she pretended to be.

The card gave an address in Meadows Lane. "I have not driven much in London this past year, and before that, I was traveling. Where is Meadows Lane?" he asked. "I do not recall the name."

"It is not far from the park. I shall send you directions.

"And now," she said, changing the subject abruptly, "I greatly fear that I must get on with my errands. If you would be so kind as to drop me in Bond Street?"

Matthew gave his driver the word, and they had soon pulled over in front of a millinery Faye had pointed out. At the end of his weakened resources for the day, Matthew did not argue when she insisted she would find her way home. He only prayed he would not regret the rash impulse that had led him to accept her mad proposal.

Chapter Five

The next few days were restless ones for Matthew. Instead of sending him back to his bed, the outing had made him eager for more activity. Nothing was harder for a man of his enterprise than to sit idle once a fire had been lit inside him. And suddenly one burned. Ambition, which had always been at the crux of his character, had sprung back to life with the thought of facing his accusers with an ally by his side. Not the same dark ambition that had driven him into Africa, but one that was much more fundamental: the desire to restore his reputation in the eyes of his peers.

True, Ahmad had always been his willing supporter. But no matter how enlightened the patrons of the African Association were, they were still Englishmen and full of bias. To them Ahmad was nothing more than a specimen of his race. A particularly fine one, but merely an object for study, certainly not a man whose opinion they would consult. After all, he had not been properly brought up, nor had he attended the proper English university. So how could he be believed?

The narrow minds of Matthew's colleagues made

Faye's liberality seem all the more remarkable. That her girl's mind should hold more wisdom than all those learned brains put together confounded him, but her belief in him somehow meant even more to him than Ahmad's steadfast friendship. And Matthew was not so foolish as to think it was because Faye was merely one of his own kind.

Discovering within himself a distinct impatience to see her again, he sent her a note informing her of the time of the association's next meeting and asking where he should call to take her up. Her response arrived on Saturday when he and Ahmad were passing through the plain entryway of their apartments in the wake of their afternoon meal. Matthew slit open the seal of her missive, doing his best to conceal his eagerness.

However, when he read Faye's reply, excusing herself from riding with him on the grounds that she had another engagement earlier that evening, fresh doubts made his heart sink. She would have to meet him at the tavern to arrive by the designated hour. Matthew could not help wondering whether she would appear at all.

His misgivings were ably seconded by Ahmad.

"But, Matthew saab," Ahmad said when he had been acquainted with her reply, "what do you know of this woman?"

Alerted by his friend's plaintive note, Matthew braced himself. "What does any man know of any woman?"

"Saab"—Ahmad's voice was mildly scolding—"I only ask you to beware. Do you not find it strange that she should go about all alone?"

"Eccentric perhaps, but not so out of the ordinary as to raise the degree of suspicion you obviously entertain."

Matthew felt burdened by his own suspicions—that Faye was, for whatever reason of her own, attempting to keep him from knowing where she lived. Or worse, that she had heard the rumors about him and had thought better of being seen with him. Already the prospect of facing the men who had accused him had put him on edge. He did not need an additional cause for disquiet.

Ahmad ignored Matthew's subtle plea for reassurance. "I was under the impression that unmarried English ladies would always walk out chaperoned."

"Often they do. But should they do otherwise, we do not take them out in the marketplace and stone them. And," Matthew snapped unreasonably, "if you find you are fond of such entertainment, I suggest you find another country in which to reside."

Fortunately Ahmad had experienced Matthew's sharp temper before and did not take offense. Why *would* he, Matthew asked himself, feeling contrite, when he had often in his delirium cursed Ahmad for being so inconsiderate as to jostle him while carrying him on his back through the jungle?

But when Matthew started to apologize, he saw that Ahmad was not amused as he had been on that particular occasion. Instead, his brow was heavy with concern, and his eyes flickered with a hint of fear.

"Do you know what we say in my country when a

beautiful lady appears and disappears so suddenly?" Ahmad asked.

Matthew wanted to sigh, but since he had treated Ahmad so roughly already, he merely replied, "No. What does one say?"

"We say she is one of the jinn."

Matthew had seen the notion coming. He had experienced much superstition on his travels, in all its forms, so he knew when it typically arose. When objects appeared but no one could remember how they came to be in that place. When strangers entered a village, unaccompanied and unannounced. When a plague was visited upon a people who needed someone to blame.

Except Ahmad had never been one for supernatural beliefs, aside from his Mohammedan religion, which he scrupulously observed. Long ago he had hoped to convert Matthew to his faith and had even braved the extreme sacrilege of smuggling him into Mecca disguised as a Syrian doctor in order to attain that goal.

Matthew had been sincerely sorry to disappoint him, but he had not been able to accept Ahmad's religion any more than he had the one into which he had been born. Faith had not come easily to him then, and it never would come to him now, not after all the cruelty he'd seen and the treachery he'd experienced.

And if religion would not come to him, he saw no reason to submit to fruitless superstition. He grinned at Ahmad, who retired in the face of Matthew's amused disbelief. Diverted, Matthew went up to his study to read.

It was not until he was halfway up the stairs that he recalled the elves who visited his hallucinations: Francis and Trudy. The memory of those visitors made him halt.

Strange that Ahmad should have had a suspicion so near his own feverish delirium. Matthew did not recall ever having told Ahmad about the elves.

Wondering at the bizarre coincidence, he shook his head and resumed his climb.

Whatever anxieties might have troubled him had he been forced to wait that evening, he was spared them, for Faye kept to their appointment. Not only did she arrive precisely at the stroke of midnight, but the carriage that brought her appeared in the next instant after his own.

Matthew stepped to its door with the thought of helping her down as soon as he saw her attempting to alight. But he was momentarily distracted by her horses, which turned their heads in unison as he passed them, rather like two opera dancers on a stage. They must have suspected that he had a lump of sugar in his pocket.

As Faye made her descent, however, cutting them a startled glance, they swung rapidly back to face the street, for all the world like a couple of naughty children.

"Hummph!" Ahmad was heard to grunt behind him.

Matthew chuckled at this odd equine behavior, then turned to greet Faye, who looked enchanting in a hooded, fur-trimmed pelisse. "I did not know you kept a carriage," he said.

"Yes." Excitement raised roses in her cheeks. "It is quite new. Do you admire it?"

Matthew obliged her by looking it over as well as he could in the lamplight. He had already noticed Faye's penchant for gold and glistening materials, so he told himself he should not be surprised by the quantity of gilt on the wheels.

Even so, he was. Such luxury was seldom indulged except by persons of enormous fortune, and nothing Faye had ever said had led him to believe her father had been that wealthy. Gentlemen who sought occupation in the diplomatic service were rarely men of great wealth, but perhaps Faye had withheld some part of her father's history. Perhaps he had been a nabob after all.

As quickly as these thoughts flitted through his brain, Matthew responded, "I think it a quite remarkable conveyance. It rather . . . shines."

Faye peeked out from beneath her hood, and her enthusiasm began to fade. "Do you think it much too vulgar?"

"Nothing you've chosen could possibly be vulgar," Matthew reassured her, unsettled by her dismay and amazed to find within himself the gallantry to address it. He had always been curt and abrupt, much too busy to consider another person's feelings. But the impulse to comfort Faye had come quite naturally.

He offered her his arm to escort her in. But just then another figure as delicate as Faye's emerged from the carriage.

In response to his questioning look, Faye said, "I thought I should bring my maid."

Normally that explanation would have sufficed, but Matthew could not bring himself to ignore Faye's maid. She was curiously dressed in a cloak of uncommon luxury, which had all the appearance of cashmere. Before Matthew could ponder the question of whether this was evidence of Faye's rash generosity or rather proof of the same vain impulse that had led her to gild the wheels of her carriage, he noted the girl's stunning face, and it riveted his eye.

The maid was every bit as lovely as Faye, with golden blond hair of a satin fineness. She had sapphire-blue eyes, the color so intense, it was visible even in dim lantern light. She raked him up and down with a bold glance before ruining her marvelous impression by raising one hand and dissolving in a fit of giggles.

"Grace!" The anguished reminder from Faye had almost no effect on the girl, who gave her mistress a sullen glance before resuming her open flirtation.

If Grace had adorned the drawing rooms of London, she would have been considered a diamond of the first water, no matter how appallingly forward her manners might be. As it was—even considering her low degree of birth—Matthew had no doubt she had a promising chance of becoming the city's most famous courtesan.

"Saab—" Ahmad's voice came from behind him, stern and full of warning.

Matthew tore his glance away from the girl, aware that Faye, too, was awaiting him anxiously, which made him wonder why on earth she had ever employed the girl. Grace's charms posed no danger to

him, but it would be very hard to keep follow-
ers from gathering about her, especially when it
appeared that the bold piece would give them every
encouragement.

"Shall we go in?" Matthew ignored Ahmad's
attempts to meet his eye.

Frustrated, the big Pathan waited for them all to
pass before following them.

As Matthew and Faye turned their backs on
Grace to head inside, he felt a distinct relaxation on
Faye's part.

"I thought the gentlemen of the African Association would take it amiss if I appeared unchaperoned
with you," Faye whispered, "else I would never have
brought Grace. I am terribly afraid she is not civilized enough to be taken into polite company."

Matthew had no time to ponder this strange
remark for they were inside and had other, more
immediate matters to face.

With this moment finally upon them, he felt a
resurgence of some of his former strength. The same
unflinching courage that had allowed him to look
death in the face every day for two long years made
him lengthen his stride now.

What, frankly, could happen to him as a result of
this night's business, except that the members
might attempt to have him expelled? And since they
had tried that once already, what more did he have
to lose?

Faye's dainty fingers on his arm had infused him
with a churning confidence, and he somehow knew
that no degree of disgust on his enemies' part would
deter her from her mission. As they entered the hall

of the tavern, which led to the private dining room, he could feel her support in the faint squeeze she gave his arm. When he peered down, she gave him a wink so full of conspiratorial mischief as to make him eager to see the scene ahead.

Grace was told to stay outside in the corridor with the serving men. His arms folded on his chest, Ahmad glowered at her from the corner. As soon as Matthew turned his back on them, he heard her chair being surrounded by the serving men who were waiting nearby for their masters' orders. A rippling giggle behind him made him hope Grace would not become so loud as to distract the members.

In the private dining room, a long table had been set for numerous courses. By this late hour—one Matthew had chosen for its particular effect—the covers had all been removed and various bottles had been scattered around. The gentlemen seated about the table, stiff in their evening garb, had pushed back their chairs and unfastened their bottom waistcoat buttons the better to discuss business over their port.

Sir Joseph Banks, president of the Royal Society and founder of this immediate body, sat at the head of the assembly. He was himself an explorer who had traveled with Captain Cook, and on the strength of his contributions to science, he had been made a baronet and received the Order of the Bath. As Matthew heard the first astonished mumblings from those who had remarked his entrance, it was to Sir Joseph that he looked. Whatever feelings the president displayed upon seeing him would prevail with the members, no matter what their personal opinions might be.

Wariness lit the venerable gentleman's eye before he stood, followed by the others. Matthew heard a muttered oath, then a curse.

"Dunstone?" Sir Joseph's utterance of his name seemed a challenge rather than a greeting. Matthew felt the muscles in his stomach knot.

"Sir Joseph." He did his best to keep an even tone.

Then, out of the corner of his eye, Matthew saw Sir Julian Speck, and his jaw tightened, making it impossible for him to speak. Hostility raised the hairs on the back of his neck.

Matthew stared at his well-dressed rival. The tips of Speck's starched shirt points reached as high as his wine-flushed ears. A waistcoat in rich ivory brocade covered the unmistakable beginnings of a paunch. The fury that had been accumulating in Matthew for these past many painful months emerged from the ash where it had been banked. Matthew held his fire in check but felt it burning in his eyes.

Speck's glance wavered, but he hid his discomfort behind a twitching sneer.

A tense silence hovered in the room, waiting only for someone to break it. Much as he knew that person had to be himself, Matthew felt chagrin freezing his mouth and anger blocking his speech. In his wealth of emotions he had almost forgotten the dainty creature at his side when Faye threw back the hood of her pelisse, and the gentlemen gasped.

With a grin suddenly tickling at his lips, Matthew

released his adversary's gaze. Instead of the paralysis he had known just moments ago, he experienced a boyish rush of triumph. With one look at Faye's beautiful, spritelike face, these gentlemen, who had wished to hang Matthew in effigy if not in earnest, seemed at once to have forgotten all their animosity.

"Sir Joseph," Matthew said, breaking their trance, "allow me to present Miss Faye Meriwether to your members. Miss Meriwether has come with a plea she believes will appeal to their generosity of spirit."

Ignoring the wryness in Matthew's tone, Sir Joseph stepped forward to lead her to his place at the head of the table, giving Matthew the luxury to reflect. If he had attempted to foist anyone else upon the group, either he or she would have been suspected from the outset. But no one raised a word of protest about the woman who had invaded their proceedings. Instead, the members all stared at Faye, their eyes bulging from their heads. Matthew would have stepped back, the better to enjoy the effect of her particular magic, but a determined grip of her fingers on his arm kept him near her side.

"Gentlemen . . ."

At Faye's first word, Matthew felt the air about him shiver with delight. So mesmerized were the men, they forgot to offer her a seat but, instead, stood frozen in place while she told them of her charity.

Watching her now and feeling the power of the spell she wove, Matthew could not help but recall Ahmad's remark. It was no wonder his friend thought her a jinni, when she possessed so much magnetism as to make the very air about her hum. Faye made an impassioned plea on behalf of the almshouse, and one by one the gentlemen nodded as if their heads were strung like marionettes'. Matthew could almost see the guineas flying from their purses.

"I have to thank Sir Matthew Dunstone for bringing me to see you and for his own generosity in our cause," Faye said. She pressed herself against his arm, and he felt a radiant glow. "Sir Matthew, having so bravely traveled the globe himself, knows how terrifying it is to be abandoned in a foreign country, and because of this he has taken a compassionate interest in our inmates."

At her use of the word "abandoned," Matthew started. He glanced rapidly at the men's faces, certain he would discover a similar shock. Sir Julian Speck had certainly gone whiter against his cravat, but none of the others seemed to have noticed the irony of Faye's remark. It was as if they had completely forgotten Speck's accusations and the scandal Matthew had caused when he'd returned to refute them. Instead, the few who had been able to tear their gazes away from Faye were staring at Matthew with a newfound respect.

Matthew frowned, uncertain whether Faye's remark had been the result of mere chance or if she had heard of his quarrel with Speck and had espoused his side. He had to wonder if he had let something slip to expose the injury that had been done to his reputation. However, when he looked down at her, he found no evidence of any particular knowledge of those distressing events. Faye was instead beaming up at him with an adoring look in her eye, as if he were the author of all her happiness.

A jolt, like lightning, ripped through him. Even if she was smiling at him only for dramatic effect, that smile was so damned effective as to make him wish devoutly it were real.

And the reason for his colleagues' respect was now plainly obvious to him. It was the result of pure male envy.

Under the spell of her admiration, Matthew felt his pride swelling to the point of bursting. Certain he had colored up, he forced himself to look away. He saw a similar discomfort on the faces of the other gentlemen, who burned with such covetousness as to perspire. Even Sir Julian, who had great reason to fear if Matthew were reinstated in the group, seemed to have overlooked that threat, so overwhelmed was he by the sight of her face.

Faye seemed to sense that she had stirred these gentlemen to the boiling point. She lowered her eyes, and the frenzied heat Matthew had felt in the room began to fade.

"Sir Joseph"—she smiled at the great man, and he almost seemed afraid to be singled out—"if you would permit, I should like to speak with each and every gentleman present to hear how much he would care to give."

With his instant permission Faye made a slow round of the table, pausing to take each gentleman by the hand. Matthew followed closely behind her, watching each one's reaction and marveling at her technique. With those mesmerizing green eyes turned away from him, he was better able to see how she managed it, but still he did not entirely understand how she produced the effect.

A beautiful face, so rare in its perfection as to draw all eyes, was certainly a major part of her magic. A musical voice made everyone wish to hear her speak and be anxious to acquiesce. But there was some other ingredient—some strange, elusive quality Matthew had never experienced in all his travels that troubled him nearly as much as it attracted him.

Suppressing that nagging sense of worry, he cursed himself as an ungrateful wretch. Whatever her magic was, he should only be thankful for it now, for the members of the African Association seemed to have forgotten their quarrel with him. As soon as she passed Sir Joseph, he shook Matthew's hand and inquired after his health, welcoming him back to their proceedings. Matthew even got the distinct impression that Sir Joseph had begun to c Speck's story, an impression reinforced by e other member in turn.

It was not until Faye reached Sir Julian Speck that her spell was broken. Something in his nervous glances, the fear that made him lick his lips, or the resentment that caused him to look on her with suspicion alerted her to the fact that he was the source of Matthew's pain.

Trudy paused and checked Matthew's face, where she found once again the tension that had accompanied them into the room. Instinct prodded her to play a trick upon this Speck human, to tweak his nose at the very least, but Matthew's strong determined stare gave her pause.

Matthew's reluctance to discuss the cause of his embarrassment was something she had never come across. Certainly elves who had been wronged were never known for their reserve, and the humans she had seen seldom behaved that much better.

Matthew, on the other hand, seemed to prefer to manage his own affairs. Filled with a sudden pride in him, Trudy sensed she should let him handle this man his own way.

With a sense of discretion she did not know she possessed, she posed the same questions to Sir Julian that she had to all the other men. Only a certain frost in her tone conveyed her displeasure to him, and a spark in her eye—a very real spark—made him wince.

The tour of the room complete, they had only to bid their hosts good night and retire. Trudy knew the gentlemen would have liked to ask her to stay, but such an invitation would have been most improper—certainly every bit as improper as her appearance at their meeting in a tavern had been.

Besides, she felt anxious to discover what mischief Grace had been up to during their absence. It wouldn't have surprised Trudy one bit if Grace had led Ahmad into the mists and destroyed all her plans.

Fortunately she and Matthew had not been gone long enough for Grace to become bored by the numerous swains who had gathered about her. Serving men quite cluttered the hall despite all Ahmad's admonishments, the strength of which

Trudy and Matthew heard as they approached. Trudy regretted having exposed these poor, unfortunate footmen to her cousin, but she had overheard Ahmad's concerns that afternoon as she had hidden in Matthew's house, and she had been desperate to produce some proof of her respectability. Nothing could have served so well as a maid, but involving her scapegrace of a cousin was bound to be a risk.

"Grace," she scolded, trying to sound the part of an offended mistress though she ached to pinch her wayward cousin, "I am astonished by your behavior. I insist you go outside at once."

Grace made an impudent face and flounced out the door.

All the footmen she'd enchanted would have followed her blindly if Matthew had not quickly stepped between them and the exit. One curt word from him, however, and they dispersed.

Once Grace had been bustled into the carriage, Matthew turned back to Trudy and grinned with one eyebrow raised. "If I were you," he suggested, "I should find that girl a husband."

"I should, if I thought it would make any difference." Trudy sighed. "But I fear she would continue to put me to the blush."

He cocked her a glance. "Then why on earth do you employ her?"

"Oh . . ." Trudy groped for a logical answer and found one. "You would be surprised, I daresay, but not many respectable girls wish to be employed in a house headed by a woman. They are as mistrustful of their own sex as most men."

"People can be fools." Matthew seemed troubled.

"But I beg, if you have any difficulty at all in finding the servants you need, you must let me assist you."

His offer brought a rush to her cheeks, an unexpected warmth, as if she had intercepted a ray from the sun.

But before she could respond, he captured her hand, and she experienced a deeper heat, more intense even than before.

"Thank you for coming with me this evening."

"Not at all," she protested, breathless. "It is I who should thank you—for my society—"

"Damn your society."

Startled, Trudy caught her breath. She knew she should express virtuous outrage, but she also knew too well what he meant. So, instead, she dimpled and was rewarded by his grin.

Matthew's dark stare made her stomach churn with a mysterious swirling that made her head go dizzy.

"At least for the moment," he said, "I'd like to forget your most noble experiment to speak of something more immediate to me. If I hadn't seen it, I wouldn't have believed how envy, no matter how premature"—with a quick blink, he corrected himself—"no matter how *misplaced*, could influence a group of intelligent men. I don't know how the devil you managed it, but with one stroke you have given me a chance I never thought to have again."

"And what will you do with that chance?" With a stab of fierce worry, she said, "Surely, you don't mean to set out for Africa again? There must be far safer places to explore."

Matthew shook his head. "I doubt I shall ever be

fit for that much adventure again," he said. With a frown, he cloaked his thoughts.

Trudy wondered what he might have said if she had not been so hasty with her foolish outburst. What reason did she have to worry over Matthew? She would soon be showing him those "safer places" she had mentioned, and once she had him there, he would most likely forget all he'd known or wanted in this world.

She considered leading him into the mists right now, now that he felt so grateful to her. But something stayed her and with a start she realized it was because she did not want to. She'd felt so happy of late. These past few days while she had been playing with Matthew and plotting all the many ways to help him, she had managed to forget her own restlessness. This unanticipated contentment, spiced with a healthy dose of excitement, felt so good, she would not be in a hurry to give it up.

And besides, Christmas was still two weeks away, which would give her plenty of time to win her wager with Francis.

Trudy had forgotten that Ahmad was waiting for his friend, but now the big Pathan came to loom beside them. She offered to deliver them to their door, but Ahmad spoke for them both.

"I have already taken the liberty of ordering Matthew saab a chair, and if he does not object, I shall enjoy the walk beside him."

Matthew started to protest, but a look at Ahmad's face stopped him. The unfamiliar tension between them made Trudy feel dismay. Ahmad's concern for his friend was well placed, and for that reason, she supposed, it made her feel guilty for the second time in her life.

Fearful of something she couldn't define, Trudy bid them both good night. Then, with a stern eye on her two "horses," both of whom had been shamelessly eavesdropping, she let Matthew hand her up, only hoping that her neighing relatives would behave long enough to pull the carriage out of his sight.

Chapter Six

That night Matthew was beset by visions more tangled than ever before. All the usual strange and frightening ingredients were there: the endless sands, stretching for miles and miles between oases; the punishing heat; the desperate need to shield himself from the eyes of Mohammedans eager to kill the faithless infidel. Then in a shift of scenery from burning sand to dark, wet forest, he beheld bizarre ritualistic practices, the likes of which his English world had never seen; the violation of women; the torture of men.

But in this dream Helen was there, and with her husband, Sir Julian Speck, though Speck had never stayed with the expedition long enough to witness these last delights. Speck sat near the source of the Nile mounted on a camel with Helen perched side-saddle on the animal's curved neck.

Both were elegantly dressed for a ball. Both looked down their haughty noses at him. They had the same golden hair, though Sir Julian's locks had been heavily groomed with pomade.

Matthew knelt anxiously before them in Mohammedan robes, his beard black and thick and itching.

Chains weighed heavily on his wrists, and perspiration coursed down his cheeks. His feet were manacled, too, and he could feel the pain of countless slaves in the wounds that oozed upon his back.

He could sense the threat Sir Julian posed: his jealousy, his ignorance, and his scorn.

"The man you have captured is not the Syrian doctor he would have you believe," Sir Julian intoned.

Matthew did not have to peer behind him to see the ferocity of his captor, a cannibal chief. His body would be scarred by self-imposed wounds, his hair slicked down by elephant fat, and his eyes eerily emptied of a soul. What man could retain his soul who had killed as ruthlessly and as often as this chieftain had?

"Helen . . ." Matthew tried to beg her for mercy, but his throat was constricted by chains.

"Lud, Matthew! What gibberish is this?" Helen smiled and rapped her fan on the camel's head. "I do not speak Arabic, sir, and I will thank you not to assault my ears with it."

"Do not tell them who I am," Matthew pleaded.

Sir Julian smiled at the chief with sneering condescension. "Who is this? Why, he's the famed Sir Matthew Dunstone, explorer and linguist. Madman. Infidel. And my former partner. Tragic, isn't it, that he should have lost his mind."

The chains were tightened around Matthew's neck until he could scarcely breathe. His robes were stripped from him. And even though desert winds were chafing the skin from his cheeks, the jungle moisture made him shiver at the thought of the death to come.

He had seen many such deaths. Seen and witnessed them in silence for fear of losing his own life. What did it matter that he had saved the lives of the chieftain's children with simple remedies from home, when they would live to perpetuate the cruelties of their sire?

"Helen . . ." Matthew tried to croak out the word, but Helen's golden image faded as the blackness swamped him and his whole body was racked with pain.

"Mannie?" Trudy hovered over his face again. "Can ye hear me? Are ye quite all right, my mannie?"

Matthew closed his eyes and let her voice waft through him. Her breath upon his face soothed his raging fever like a cool, welcome breeze.

"Trudy," he breathed, awash with joy and relief.

"That's right." She seemed pleased that he'd remembered her name. "Ye know me this time, don't ye."

"You're not that easy to forget. I don't know many elf maids."

"Well, take it from me that I'm the best."

He chuckled, but the memory of his nightmare was still deep inside his flesh, and he shuddered again.

"I've got a question for ye, mannie." Her voice pulled him back from the dark.

"What?" He wanted her to keep on talking, no matter how great a fool he was to listen.

"Why are ye so sad? Why do ye sit in yer chair when ye ought to be out and about?"

"I'm too ill."

"Aye. That ye are sometimes, mannie, but not always. Why don't ye go out when yer well?"

"And frighten all the women and children with my wild ravings? It would be cruel."

"Yer teasing me, mannie."

"That I am. Although . . ."

He had been branded a lunatic. Until this evening when Faye had used her incredible charm to reinstate him with his colleagues, he'd thought he would forever more be considered mad. Either that or a coward. And now that he was trembling from fever, he could not be sure such a scene had truly transpired. How could it? There had been something distinctly fantastic about the whole episode: the gilt on Faye's coach, Grace's incomparable beauty, and the pair of horses one would have sworn had laughed. Nothing had seemed real, in fact, but Sir Julian's sneer and Faye's cool reception of him, as if she had guessed the part he had played in Matthew's ruin. And then, before they'd departed, when she had pleaded with him not to make another hazardous journey.

"Faye does not seem to be frightened of me," he said aloud unconsciously.

"Does that please ye?" Trudy's prying voice reminded him of her presence on his bed.

"I suppose." He was done with being too honest with Trudy. How strange to be embarrassed by the teasing of his own illusion. But she seemed so real.

"If ye thought she was pretty, then ye ought to go find her, don't ye think?"

"To what end?" He curled his lips in a derisive smile. "To impress her with my strength?"

"Ye don't look so weak to me."

"I am a shadow of my former self. I have heard it whispered many times."

"By who?"

"By all the tabbies."

"Sure, and do ye mind what a bunch of females say?"

"And by the Toms." No, he did not mind so much what the ladies said, for they would insist on repeating what they'd heard from others. But that his colleagues should be such idiots . . .

"Tell me, mannie. Tell me what those ignoramuses say that bothers you."

Matthew smiled. He had two champions now, it seemed: one in real life and one in his dreams.

He opened his eyes, and the temptation to touch Trudy was almost painful. He wished he could draw her down to lie curled upon his chest and warm him. Matthew willed his shaking hands to stay at his sides. He would not go chasing after phantoms.

He let his eyelids droop again. With his eyes closed, her presence was more soothing than tempting. He answered her question in his head.

I do not go out because I cannot bear the angry stares of people who once looked at me with awe. I cannot bear to be the object of their gossip or their pity or their scorn.

Feverish as he was, Matthew did not realize he had spoken his thoughts aloud in Arabic until Trudy answered him in the same tongue.

"Why do they pity you?"

Somehow it was easier to voice these things aloud in a foreign language, almost as if his secrets were still hidden and his identity were still concealed.

"Only some of them pity me. Those are the ones who think I went mad somewhere in the interior of Africa. The others, who are not so charitable, think I turned coward and abandoned my partner in the desert rather than fight."

Trudy's voice trembled. "Why do they think that?"

Matthew opened his eyes again and saw the growing consternation in hers. Obviously she wanted him to absolve himself.

Might as well tell her the truth.

In his illness and his pride, he'd refused to argue for his name. He'd refused to raise proof against the charges thrown in his face by the African Association, whose members had swallowed the whole of Sir Julian Speck's lies. So no one had known—no one but his faithful Ahmad, who had stayed with him throughout all his travails.

Matthew had tried to tell himself that one person was enough; his one true friend knew the truth. But he had never been able to get over the bitterness of Speck's betrayal, his colleagues' willingness to believe his partner-turned-rival, and Helen's defection. He had been too ill to fight them all, and much too proud to complain without fighting. But here, in the privacy of his own bedroom, surely he could set the record straight.

"They believe I abandoned my partner to the mercies of a band of cutthroats in order to save my own skin."

"And why would they believe such a wicked lie?"

"It is what my partner told them."

Matthew reached one hand slowly toward her face. So engrossed was she in their discussion that she permitted him to stroke it, and the feel of her skin, so much like rose petals, melted something inside him.

"Why did he do such a thing?" she whispered.

She didn't doubt him. She was his creation, so of course she shouldn't, but he'd been betrayed by his dreams before.

Still, her faith in him made him sigh, and inside it felt as if a piece of rock had been chiseled away. "Because that was precisely what he did to me," Matthew said.

A moment passed before she understood him. When she did, she recoiled and her forehead wrinkled. "Bah!"

It was an explosive sound, which surprised him for its honesty, for he was not accustomed to such noises from females.

In recoiling, Trudy had broken away from his touch, but she hardly seemed to realize he had been stroking her, so angry was she. "That Speck ought to be hanged!"

Matthew grinned. His champion was as fragile as a nymph, but he was glad to have her on his side. She seemed to double his own strength. "They don't hang men for destroying another man's reputation."

"Well, they should!"

"Perhaps. I won't quarrel with you on that point."

"Then you should confront him," Trudy said. "Make him change his story."

He closed his eyes again. Matthew expected a

wave of exhaustion to engulf him, as one had every time he had considered such an action. But, surprisingly, he did not feel defeated this time. Instead, an urge of sorts had taken birth inside his chest.

"Confront him?" he said, blinking at Trudy. "If I do that, I should as well confront his wife."

Confusion, then suspicion, spread over Trudy's face. She cocked her head warily. "And why, my mannie, should ye want to talk to his wife?"

If—Matthew told himself in that moment—he were not such a rational creature, he just might believe that the elf maid he'd conjured was jealous.

"I was engaged to marry Sir Julian's wife when I left on my final expedition," he explained. "When I returned, I found she had married my rival."

"Yer much better off without her!" Trudy exclaimed with a toss of her head.

She *was* jealous. Matthew fought an unreasoning grin. He must be a lunatic after all.

"Undoubtedly," he said to soothe her temper. "That does not mean I wasn't a bit perturbed at the time."

Trudy quieted, but her eyes still held a wary glint. "Have ye forgotten all about her, then?"

"I—" Matthew struggled to make his feelings clear. "I suppose I have forgotten my love for her, if I ever did love her, but it is harder to get over her betrayal."

"Ye can do it, mannie!" Trudy said anxiously. "All ye have to do is think of Faye. If you just follow her—"

Matthew's sudden look of offense made her stop. Trudy realized she had used the wrong words where

Matthew was concerned. All his life he had been the one to lead, never to follow.

In that moment Trudy understood what Francis had meant when he had said Matthew would not be pixie-led. She began to have doubts, her first real doubts, that she could lead this man into the mists to be hers. And the oppressiveness of those doubts seemed greater, far greater than they should be if all that concerned her was losing a wager.

Silence fell between them until Matthew reached out a hand to touch her cheek once again. Trudy flinched as if she'd been burned. She scooted to the foot of the bed, scolding him in a breathless voice, "Not so fast. Not so fast."

She was pleased by the frustration she saw in Matthew's eyes.

"Mannie," she breathed in a coaxing whisper, "why don't ye let Faye help ye to forget yer hurts?"

"She does help me to forget them." Matthew's gaze hazed over, and she thought he must be remembering her as Faye, which gave her hope.

"There, ye see," she said. "Then forget all them others. Who needs them when ye've got her?"

"Have I got her?" Matthew was speaking to himself. "I don't know. . . ."

"Of course ye have. Ye've only got to make up yer mind."

He shook his head with a frown, and some emotion gripped her heart.

"What's wrong?"

"It's Faye herself. . . . She's almost too perfect . . . as if she could not be real. . . ."

Anxiety gripped Trudy's stomach. "Don't ye like her, mannie? Don't ye admire her?"

"Of course I do. She's beautiful and courageous and loyal—so close to my dreams. But—"

"But what?"

"But when I think of reaching for her, all I suspect I will find in my arms is thin air."

Trudy sucked in a sudden breath. How could he know? Did her mannie know everything?

For the first time in her life, she felt awed by a respect for humankind. No. This was not the first time. The first had been when she'd been standing between Matthew and his rival and she'd felt Matthew's strength beside her and she'd known that he would deal with his enemy when he wished—in his own way.

There was something at the core of Matthew that she could sense but did not have herself. It was the same something he felt was missing in Faye but could not put a name to. That something was a soul.

If Trudy could sense the soul in Matthew, then it made sense he would feel its lack in Faye, but this was something she had not figured on. Neither had she realized how much this bit of knowledge would hurt.

She made an attempt to distract herself with a laugh. "Put that other woman behind ye, mannie, and see if Faye don't seem better to ye then."

Matthew was silent. By the worried look on his face, she suspected he was as troubled by his failure to love Faye as she was. He simply did not understand it, whereas she most painfully did. How could he guess that his newfound friend, who dressed the way a lady should and spoke such elegant English as to seem to the manor born, was an elf?

"Shall I sing to ye, mannie?" Trudy ventured in a shaking voice.

The wrinkles on his brow disappeared, and he sighed as he closed his eyes. "Yes, please sing to me, pretty maid."

Trudy scooted forward toward his pillow. "If ye promise not to grab me, I'll stroke yer forehead for ye. That'll make ye get well quick."

"Then by all means I give my promise not to touch you."

A little ache spread in Trudy's chest. It grew much worse. "I'll let ye touch me someday, mannie, I promise. Just not now."

In the morning Matthew felt completely renewed, as if the magic in his dream maiden's fingertips had worked. He could still feel the tenderness of Trudy's dainty hands upon his face and neck. His reaction to the memory of her touch was strong enough to embarrass him. For a grown man to be enamored of a delusion was patently ridiculous. But he could not shake the feeling that her hands had been real and that they had gently stroked his skin until his fever had vanished and the muscles of his arms and legs had flexed with new strength.

He also could not let go of the certainty that it was time now to face the people who had wronged him. With his physical powers in some measure restored, he would have the resources to deal with a confrontation. And he knew that to go on with his life, he must bury the aches of the past.

Trudy's probing questions about Faye and his feelings for her had disturbed him more than he liked to think. There was no question in his mind that Faye, with her youth, enthusiasm, and faith, had been the inspiration for his comforting dreams and the true basis for his healing.

He was grateful to her. More than that, he was fascinated by her, so much so that he wondered if she might not be the answer to all his troubles. Since she had appeared in his library unannounced, his life had taken a sudden change. For the first time in years, he felt glowingly alive.

Faye had proven her good faith by supporting him in front of his colleagues. Though the effects of her magic on those gentlemen would surely wear off, at least he now had a chance to go up against them on a fair playing field, unhampered by a stiff, unreasoning defense. For this, not to mention her countless other virtues, he ought to love her.

Why, then, was he unable to trust her as he should?

Until last night Matthew had not put into words the concerns that had troubled him about Faye, uppermost that eerie, unsettling feeling that she might vanish just as suddenly as she had come. Whether a result of Ahmad's superstition or of his own disorientation as caused by his delusions, he knew such a fear was absurd. But knowing this did not help to diminish it.

Perhaps his unwillingness to believe in her was due to Helen's unfaithfulness and the resulting harm it had caused.

If that were the case, he had best resolve the

lingering hurt from that past experience, else he would risk losing the greatest gift ever to come his way.

Leaving Ahmad behind at home, Matthew decided to walk the few blocks to Sir Julian's residence in Audley Street. The crisp December air was bracing, and the fir and holly hanging everywhere put him in mind of his ride in the park with Faye. He remembered how dull he had felt then, only a short time past, and how her daring had awakened him. She was every bit as courageous in her own way as he had been when he'd first set out on his travels.

No more than fifteen minutes brought him to Sir Julian's door. His knock was answered by a footman who instantly recognized Sir Matthew Dunstone and, remembering the scene Matthew had made on a former occasion, hastily informed him that neither his master nor mistress was at home.

Matthew, who knew both of their habits very well, had no trouble deciphering this message. When he asked if he might come in to leave a note, the footman sought to close the door in his face.

Matthew put one hand out to prevent him and forced the door ajar. For this simple maneuver he needed a measure of strength, and he was happy to find that he had at least this much.

Speaking calmly, he managed to gain the footman's ear long enough to say, "Please tell your mistress that Sir Matthew Dunstone has called to pay his respects. And if she has no wish to receive me, I promise to go away."

"It'll be more'n my job is worth, sir, if I let you in."
As he pressed on the door, the footman's face grew quite red.

"I imagine it would be if I behaved the way I did last time I called, but I assure you that will not happen again."

The rationality of his speech seemed to work, and the footman relaxed his grip on the door very slightly. Matthew gave a sign of faith by removing his hand.

"Please inform Lady Speck that I have chosen to wait outside in the event she does not wish to see me."

With a wary cast to his shoulders, the footman acquiesced, and Matthew took a step away from the house to relax while he waited. He could not blame the footman for his inhospitality, for he remembered how loudly he had stormed the entrance of Sir Julian's house when he'd learned of Helen's defection. Even in his weakened state—and he remembered just how feeble he had felt when his anger had subsided—it had taken two footmen and Ahmad to expel him from the house.

Recalling the humiliation of that day, Matthew was surprised by how little it bothered him now.

More of Faye's influence? He gave a wondering smile.

In a few minutes the door was opened again, and the footman eyed him cautiously. "The mistress says she will receive you." He bowed. As Matthew passed him in the vestibule, the footman added, "But no tricks, mind."

"You have my solemn word."

Strange, but he felt like laughing, as if a footman's

insolence should be a matter for humor. But Matthew had suffered much worse at the hands of lower beings than this poor footman. He applauded the lad's stance.

He was shown into a drawing room he vaguely remembered as being decorated with a mixture of female furbelows and only the occasional sign of a male presence. Its fragile chairs with crimson damask had been chosen for the fashionable statement they made rather than for comfort, he discovered when he sat in one of them. Taking a look around, he wondered how differently Helen would have furnished her drawing room if she had been married to him.

Though, Matthew acknowledged with a rueful grimace, he need not have wondered. He would have insisted upon having everything his way even if it meant that Helen would have spent a great portion of her days in a room designed to please him.

Before he could ask himself the next logical question, how Faye would wish to arrange her drawing room, the door swung open, and he stood.

Helen paused on the threshold. The past few years had not changed her much. Her pale blond hair was gathered simply in a chignon, the same as he remembered it. Her eyes were still a gentle blue. The dignity of her gaze, which had first attracted him to her, seemed still to linger beneath her present wary glance. The only change Matthew could detect at all was a slight thickening at her waist and a certain heaviness to her step.

She hesitated, nervously fingering the doorknob, as if she might wish to flee.

Matthew hid his annoyance to make her a leg. It was one thing for the footman to think him a lunatic, quite another for someone who had known his kindness to fear him so.

"Helen." He invited her into the room with a questioning note.

"Matthew . . ." She moved forward to give him her hand, then withdrew it quickly. "I must admit your visit comes as a surprise."

"I am sure it does. I hope, however, that you will not find it too unpleasant. I promise you, I mean no harm. To you." He had to qualify that last statement, for she would not believe he was in charity with her husband, not after the accusations Sir Julian had made.

Helen flushed and begged him to be seated. Once they were settled across from each other, she had difficulty meeting his eye.

As the silence between them stretched, she began to speak in a wavering voice. "Julian informed me that you made an appearance at the Association meeting last Saturday."

"Yes, I did." Matthew frowned. "I confess to being somewhat surprised that he mentioned it to you, however."

"Oh, Julian and I have no secrets from each other."

"You are most fortunate," Matthew said wryly, and he saw her flush again.

"Julian said"—Helen hastened her speech—"that you had a remarkably beautiful young lady with you."

"Yes, I did. Her name is Faye Meriwether, but perhaps you have met her."

"No."

"She does not often indulge in society's pleasures, or so she tells me."

"Then it is you who are fortunate."

Helen's statement took him off guard. "I beg your pardon?" Matthew asked.

"Oh, Matthew, have you forgotten what you were like? Always so ungracious about my own desire for amusement. I am happy you have found someone who shares your taste."

Matthew was astonished to feel himself coloring up. "Oh, as to that, nothing has been settled. . . ."

"But from what Julian told me, Miss Meriwether is plainly in love with you."

The jolt of Helen's statement sent Matthew's head ringing. This was not why he had called and not the way the conversation was supposed to go. But how was it supposed to go?

"Tell me truly, Helen." He took the direct approach to clear his head. "Was that why you jilted me? Because I had no liking for balls?"

His use of such brutal words made her flinch, but she quickly squared her shoulders. "No! I would not have married Julian if I had believed you were still alive, though I am heartily glad I did. But *two years*, Matthew. Surely that was more than long enough to wait. And then when Julian came back and informed us all that he feared you had died and under what circumstances—"

At Matthew's angry look, Helen's recital broke off. She resumed, "But regardless of the circumstances,

I believed you were dead. What was I to do? Stay a spinster? Give up every chance for a life?"

"Did you not have a life without marriage?"

"Certainly not. What woman does?"

Faye does, Matthew thought, though he did not speak the words aloud, for he sensed how unfair they were. It was useless to compare Faye to Helen, even though he had not realized before what a coward Helen was. And even that last thought was grossly unfair.

Helen was neither more nor less than most of her kind. She was precisely what she had been raised to be. Whereas Faye—

Faye was as eccentric and boundless as he was.

The sudden realization that they were meant for each other elated him, and he wanted to kiss Helen for it.

Just then, however, the drawing room door flew open, and Sir Julian burst inside.

"If you have harmed one hair on her head—" He broke off at the sight of them sitting in civilized converse.

Helen's shock turned instantly to dismay. "Julian, dear—"

Matthew folded his arms and settled back into his chair. "Hello, Speck," he said with distaste.

Chapter Seven

"What do you mean by this, Dunstone?" Sir Julian stepped into the room and closed the door behind him, never taking his eyes from Matthew's face. He made the perfect picture of sartorial elegance in Brummell's dictated black. "I will not have you coming here and upsetting my wife."

Helen had risen to move near him. "It is quite all right, Julian. I do not think Matthew came to cause trouble."

"Not with you, Helen, at least." Matthew kept to his chair. "I found our conversation most illuminating, and I thank you for it."

Sir Julian's gaze flew back and forth between them, fear turning his visage white. Finding nothing in either face, however, to suggest a conspiracy, he relaxed just long enough to put his arm about Helen's shoulders and draw her to his side. "If you have had your say," he said to Matthew, "then I must ask you to leave."

"Oh, but I haven't," Matthew assured him. "One of my purposes in coming may have been to discover just why my fiancée jilted me, and that has been satisfied. But I am far from through with you."

"Why, you—"

"Please, Matthew," Helen said. "I implore you not to cause a fight."

"I am far too weak from malaria to be a worthy opponent for anyone," Matthew said, softening his voice for her sake, "and though you might not suspect it of me, I have learned enough to choose my moments wisely. You have my word, Helen, that I shall not challenge your husband. But we do have some unfinished business to discuss."

In the silence that followed his speech, Julian looked down into his wife's face, and Matthew was stunned by what he saw in that gaze: a desperate love and a stark terror of losing it.

Such blatant feelings rocked Matthew, and for an instant he almost pitied Speck. His discomposure was enough to make him repeat in an impatient voice no one could doubt, "I have given you my word."

Helen turned back to him and hid her reluctance with the dignity she had always possessed. "Then I shall leave you two alone."

Matthew stood as a courtesy as she retired. Helen's dignity, which at one time had meant so much to him, he now saw as merely well-schooled manners, not proof of the independence or courage he had believed her to possess. She was still a pleasant woman, but he was almost relieved to see her leave the room. Though, thankfully, none of his former feelings for Helen had been reawakened this morning, he did not particularly want her to hear what he had to say to her husband. From the uneasy glance Julian threw his way, Matthew could tell he felt the same.

When the door was closed behind Helen, the two men stood and faced each other. Julian was the first to look away.

"Very well, Dunstone," he said. "Let's have it out. You've got a nerve coming here, so why have you done it?"

Matthew's anger flared. "Can you truly not imagine why I've come?"

"It will be useless for us to discuss anything if you insist upon taking that tone. However, since it is the same you've always used with me, I suppose I should not be surprised to hear it."

"What the devil do you mean?"

Julian gave a short laugh before strolling to a table where wine and glasses had been set out. He poured himself a drink but, after one look at Matthew, had the sense not to offer him one.

"Such arrogance always. The great Sir Matthew Dunstone, famed explorer of the Nile."

No matter how much contempt Matthew had for Speck, his jealous words still cut.

"You were ever full of envy." That much had become evident soon after the outset of their journey together. Julian Speck had resented Matthew's ease with the natives who accompanied them, he had objected to Matthew's use of Arabic when he conversed with Ahmad, and he had derided every skill Matthew exercised that he did not himself possess.

The fact that Matthew had found such pettiness unreasonable and unforgivable had not endeared the two men to each other. He had felt his partner to be a millstone about his neck, always objecting and ever arguing about the route they should take, when Matthew's superior experience should have been the final authority. Only a few months into their expedition, they had discussed splitting up.

"Arrogance, Speck? Perhaps I do possess a degree of arrogance, but I will not be branded a coward by a man who, when the first bit of trouble arose, turned tail and left me surrounded by brigands."

"Me! It was you who ran off and left me lying alone in the middle of the desert!"

Matthew spoke through clenched teeth. "I suppose you have told that story so often you have started to believe it, but don't forget that I was there." His memories of that day were clearly etched on his mind: their camp at the oasis, the group of horsemen who had suddenly ridden out of a cloud of sand, the crackle of shots, the shouts of their porters.

"When I gave the order to attack the robbers, you held back instead and took off while the blackguards surrounded me."

Julian sneered. "You will have to do better than that, I'm afraid. You saw I'd been wounded, yet you and that heathen friend of yours turned and ran."

"Ahmad is not a heathen," Matthew said, taking a threatening step forward, "as you know perfectly well, for you saw him at his devotions every day, twice a day, quite unlike either you or me. But I see that this is how you twist the truth."

The scorn in Matthew's voice made the other man flinch. With a quivering hand, Julian raised his glass to his mouth and tossed it off. After a moment of silence, he bowed his head, not meeting Matthew's gaze. "My apologies to Ahmad. Whatever the quarrel between us, I should not have said what I did."

Matthew was more astonished by this admission than he'd been when he'd seen the love for Helen on Julian's face. In his anger at them both, Matthew had assumed that his rival had stolen his fiancée out of spite, and it was unsettling to discover the reverse: that perhaps Julian's desire for Helen had been the cause of all the trouble between them.

"What became of the porters?"

Julian started, a second wineglass halfway to his lips. He stared at Matthew and frowned. "They followed you. And your orders. You shouted something to them in that accursed Arabic of yours, and they rode off with all the horses."

A sudden thought took Matthew's breath away. "I gave the order to attack. They disappeared."

The two men stared at each other, both thunderstruck. Matthew could not doubt that Julian's astonishment was as genuine as his own.

He thought back again to the scene at their camp, to the confusion reigning. Had he given the order to attack in Arabic, a language Julian did not understand? But there had been so little time, and he had had to take command, and the porters were all Somals. . . .

He did not recall seeing Julian at all, but the winds had blown, and sand and smoke had formed a thick screen. It was possible. . . .

Matthew looked at his former partner and saw

the same doubts flickering across his face. Matthew put a hand to his brow and dug his fingertips in.

"I think you had better pour me a glass of that wine before you drink it all," he said, awash with weariness.

They sat in Helen's drawing room until well after midday, straightening out the tangle of events that had come between them. Julian, it appeared, had taken a ball in the shoulder almost as soon as the fighting had commenced, and since he had been within sight of Matthew at the time, he had assumed he'd been seen.

But Matthew's attention had been entirely taken up by the marauders, and by the time he had given a glance back at the camp, the air had been too thick to penetrate.

He and Ahmad had been surrounded, struck down, and led off in chains to a rebel village from which they ultimately had escaped. Julian had awakened to find everyone gone, the camp in shambles, and the horses either stolen or frightened off. Weakened by a loss of blood, he had tried to make his way on foot and had fortunately come across a caravan heading for the coast. Matthew had expressed such disgust for him before this misadventure as to convince Julian he had been purposely left to die.

He had sailed for England, where he had let it be known that Matthew had deserted him to go on alone. Then, when Matthew had never returned, it was assumed he had died somewhere in the interior.

Matthew *had* gone on, months later, determined

to find the source of the Nile even without his instruments or his guides. He and Ahmad had traveled by whatever means they could devise, in whatever guise was needed, but they had failed. Months of captivity at the court of a native chief, heat, exhaustion, and disease had defeated them. Matthew had barely made it back alive.

And now to discover that all his hatred and the fury that had kept him in bed were nothing more than the result of a bitter misunderstanding . . .

A painful restlessness finally drove him out of Julian's house, although their final words had been healing. Julian Speck had promised to do his bit to restore Matthew's reputation among the members of the African Association. The two men undoubtedly would never become friends. Matthew's erudition and arrogance were anathema to one of Sir Julian's persuasion. Julian's blatant disrespect for other cultures was infuriating to one of Matthew's keen mind. But at least they had come to terms.

The morning had taken its toll on Matthew's body. Such wrenching emotion had left him feeling limp. He needed a good dose of English mutton and some porter, he decided. So, he took himself to dine at Limmer's Hotel in Bond Street, where the conversation, which consisted of nothing but the turf, should be as innocuous as it was boring, and where a good English meal could be had.

At this early hour, he did not expect that the coffee room would be filled, so he was surprised by the noise issuing from it. Then he recalled the season, and he thought he knew the cause. Even though Christmas's ancient rituals had died out, in

England, at least, it was still an excuse for excess food and drink. And one could not indulge in the latter without other forms of revelry creeping in.

Matthew took a chair at a single table off in a dark corner and ordered himself a heavy meal. Then he sat back to watch the revelers, who laughed and took snuff and fought over their wager books.

He envied them their amusement. They had gathered here to drink with their friends and to place bets on horses. Though such companionship was something Matthew had never desired once he had turned his sights onto conquest, he felt the need of it now. The familiar smells of mutton pies and good English beer mixed with the smoke from the fire, awakening in him vague memories of scenes from his childhood, and the green of holly and ivy brought back other Yuletides.

As the old smells and sounds milled around him and his exhaustion passed, Matthew experienced a curious feeling of lightness. It was as if all his shame and anger and hatred had floated away, leaving a vast void in their place. No, not a void, precisely, but something with an elusive substance.

He wondered if in forgiving Helen and losing his hatred for Julian Speck he had not experienced a rebirth of his soul. Often in his darkest hours he'd feared that he had lost it and that it would never return. But truth and clarity had worked their inevitable magic to bring it back to life, even though its return left him still feeling relatively hollow.

An unreasonable sadness hovered over him, as if all his purpose for being had gone. If those vicious emotions had been all that had kept him alive this past year, he was an object for pity indeed.

Never one to accept a bad condition tamely, he thought about what he must do to rectify his. Find something else to care about, that was sure. But what?

He could never mount another expedition. To do so would be to court certain death. Too many men had died already in a similar search for glory for him to think otherwise, and Matthew was no fool. He had already spent his allotment of vitality in his own vain searches.

Was that his trouble? Did his failure to find the source of the Nile weigh so heavily on him, or without massive ambition was he just another man set adrift?

His dinner came, and Matthew cut off his musings, which had done nothing to soothe his disquiet. He needed action to take his mind off these dismal reflections, if not some other form of comfort entirely.

He thought of Faye, who had helped him overcome this one great tribulation of his life and who surely had the gifts to help him solve many more. And all at once he realized that with his reluctance and mistrust behind him, he was free and ready to go on with his life. A life with another woman, perhaps.

And just as suddenly he found he could no longer wait to see Faye.

After hastily eating he climbed into a hackney coach with the intention of calling upon her immediately. But when he gave the driver the name of her street, the man did not recall ever having seen a Meadows Lane near the park. Matthew suggested that he drive up and down Park Lane to look for it. The coachman told him such effort would be wasted since he knew every inch of Westminster and London as well, but Matthew insisted and in the end was disappointed.

It was always possible that a narrow lane, which was not much visited, could have been overlooked, but still the episode left him feeling vaguely uneasy. At this time of year, darkness settled very early over London, so Matthew had no recourse except to wait for the morrow. He would return home and inform Ahmad of the illuminations of the day, and next morning, he would ask for Faye at the almshouse.

Trudy had hovered about him all day, using her cloak to sneak into Helen's house and spying on them both from behind a sofa.

Though the temptation had been great to interfere, especially when either Helen or Julian had spoken sharply to Matthew, she had bitten her tongue and stayed out of his way. Matthew's expression when he had discovered his ruin had all been due to a muddled circumstance had made her wince, but there had been nothing she could do at that moment to help him. She wished she had some way of seeing him whenever she wished. Not as Trudy, but as Faye.

In the morning, after she'd divined Matthew's intentions, she flittered over to the almshouse ahead of his carriage. When he arrived, she was discussing the inmates' most pressing needs with Mr. Waite. The steward seemed to have decided not to question her infrequent appearances since they always brought some benefit to his house. And this morning he had even greeted her with a moderate indication of joy.

When Trudy saw Matthew enter the workroom where they were standing, her heart gave an astonishing leap. And her pulse kept up a flutter of rhythm even though she'd been expecting him.

Just why she should react so irrationally raised a worrisome question in her mind. But she was distracted from it when Matthew's eyes lit upon seeing her, and an answering smile sprang to her lips of its own accord.

Mr. Waite was the first to speak. "Ah, Sir Matthew. Welcome, sir. You see our dear benefactress, Miss Meriwether, has visited us again, and with quite a delightful thought in mind."

Matthew took Trudy's hand and raised it to his lips, his fixed gaze burning deeply. "Oh? And what has Miss Meriwether planned this morning?" He raised his brows as much as to say that he could see she had charmed their host at last.

Trudy let Mr. Waite speak since she thought it would appear more modest.

"She has come to ask whether our pensioners are sufficiently supplied with gloves for the winter, and I have to say they are not."

"I was afraid they could not possibly be, but that will give me something I can do for them for Christmas," Trudy said.

"Oh . . ." Suddenly uncomfortable, Mr. Waite glanced away. "If that makes the giving more acceptable to you, you may consider it as such, though of course our inmates have no use for pagan observances. Being Mohammedans for the most part, they neither drink spirits nor indulge in frivolous rites."

Matthew hid a smile and cleared his throat before offering Trudy his arm. "If Miss Meriwether is determined to celebrate the Saturnalia, perhaps I should accompany her to make certain she comes to no harm. I'm afraid the streets are rather more rowdy than usual because of the season."

As he drew her quickly out of the building, making their good-byes, Trudy protested, "The Saturnalia! I did not say I celebrated the Saturnalia!"

"No, but clearly our most-Puritan host views Christmas as a similar evil. All those pagan customs involved! The drinking and the singing and dancing must surely be viewed as wicked."

"Do you think them so?" she asked, uncertain of his temper.

Matthew laughed. "No, not at all. They are relatively harmless expressions of high spirits meant to warm us in our darkest days."

"They are much more than that," Trudy asserted.

Matthew questioned her with a glance. He had brought her to the street where his carriage waited. "And what is Christmas to you?" he asked.

Trudy flushed. "I was not necessarily speaking of Christmas," she said. "Though I am far from heathen! We have ever been—" She had been about to say that elves were Christians, too, but she doubted he would believe her.

Sensing the danger in too much speech, she ended lamely, "I was speaking of the Yule, which is different."

"How so?"

"Oh"—she gave a tiny shiver—"it is a magical time when everything is turned inside out, and goblins lurk in the dark."

Matthew's crumpled brow betrayed a hint of amusement. "Do you tell me you are superstitious, Faye?"

"Why, yes! Are not you?"

"Certainly not, and I believe you are pulling my leg." Matthew reached to open the carriage door. "Shall we go?"

"Go where?" Trudy did not wait to find out before climbing inside. Her heart had made another leap at Matthew's high spirits, as if she'd been infected by a dance.

"We are off, are we not," he asked, "to purchase gloves?"

Matthew took her to the shop where he had fitted himself out before embarking on his last expedition. A place, he assured her, where they were certain to find sturdy gloves. Trudy ordered a pair for every inmate of the almshouse and an extra one for Mr. Waite.

While she was speaking with a clerk, Matthew had a conference with the shopkeeper, who disappeared into the back of the store and came back with a box in his hands. He placed it on a table beside them and raised the lid to reveal a selection of ladies' kid gloves.

"Oh!" Trudy exclaimed as she ran her fingers lightly over the soft kid. "But they are lovely."

"I noticed," Matthew said, "that you never seem to wear gloves yourself, and I thought you might be willing to accept a gift from me."

The blood rushed from Trudy's face, and she jerked back her hand. "No, I couldn't. I must not."

"Why?" Matthew gave her a surprised and puzzled look. "Would accepting a gift from me offend your sense of propriety? I assure you it is innocently meant. I only wish to thank you for what you did at the Association meeting Saturday night."

"Oh . . ." A measure of Trudy's fear left her. This was not an attempt on Matthew's part to trap her, for he did not realize that wearing human clothes could harm an elf. Nor did he know what she was, she was certain.

Deciding the wisest move would be to accept his present without making a fuss, she thanked him very prettily and said she was very honored by his gift.

Matthew gestured to the shopkeeper to help her make her selection. But Trudy needed no help. She pointed to a pair that were as white as a new-fallen snow at midnight.

She ran her fingertips over the gloves and gave a sigh. She wondered if she could conjure anything half as soft.

"Now, if miss will try them on . . ." The shopkeeper held them out one at a time.

Again she felt as if her life was draining from her

veins. "That shan't be necessary, shall it?" Her voice croaked. "I mean, can we not simply hold them up to see if they fit?"

"Faye?" Matthew's brow was bent in a crooked line of consternation. "Is something wrong? Had you rather not have them?"

"No, no." She snatched one up. "Of course I want them. They're beautiful. It's just—"

She *did* want them very much. So much. They would be a precious gift from Matthew. He simply did not know what he asked.

Slowly and tremblingly, Trudy pulled on the gloves. She felt the immediate absence of magic in her hands. It was as if a candle had been snuffed out; a roaring fire had been thoroughly doused in just an instant. She felt helpless, as if her hands were limp.

"Do you like them?" Matthew asked, hovering by her side. "They seem a trifle large."

"Perhaps they are a mite," the shopkeeper said, "but they should do quite nicely. I had worried I would have nothing to fit such a dainty lady."

Trudy could not speak, she was so frightened. She had allowed herself to be trapped. Whatever would Francis say? What would become of her now?

Then Matthew laid his palms over hers, and both her hands tingled with life, a new sort of life. "You have such tiny hands," he whispered, taking them up in his.

His heat slowly invaded her, making its way from her fingers to her toes. The shopkeeper had discreetly whisked himself away.

Matthew dragged his palms lightly over hers

before withdrawing them entirely, and Trudy discovered she could move after all. She managed to lift her hands up before her face.

"They are lovely, Matthew," she said softly, though a mixture of fear and longing had clogged her throat and an ache had built inside her. She knew she could not remove the gloves herself. "Thank you very much."

"Would you like to keep them on?" he asked.

"No! That is, they are much too fine to wear for day. I shall save them for a special evening."

He inclined his head, then looked as if he were waiting for her to take them off.

"Could you"—she nearly choked on the request, which would seem very odd to him indeed—"that is, *would* you, please, pull them off for me?"

He hesitated a second, clearly taken aback by her forwardness. Trudy squirmed inside. She felt like a girl who'd been caught with her garters showing.

"Gladly," Matthew said, and there was no mistaking his undertone.

He slid his fingers inside one glove as he slipped it off, letting them brush the sensitive pads of her palms. The shock she got from this and the simultaneous return of her magic was enough to make her gasp. Trudy trembled all over while her second palm was subjected to the same exquisite ecstasy as the first.

As if on cue, then, the shopkeeper reappeared, and Matthew gave instructions for Trudy's gloves to be wrapped.

"And those other pairs, miss?" the shopkeeper asked.

"Oh, yes." Trudy had been so unsettled by her feelings as to forget the purpose of their errand. "I shall pay for them now." She reached in her reticule and brought forth a quantity of gold sovereigns.

The shopkeeper's eyes bulged, and even Matthew appeared disconcerted. He quickly recovered, however, and picked two coins out of the lot to place in the shopkeeper's palm. "That should be more than enough," he said. "We will wait for the change and then be off."

"We needn't wait," Trudy said, feeling anxious to be gone. "Here." She put another five pieces of gold in the man's hand.

"But, miss—"

Trudy flashed him her most generous smile. "It's the Yule. You might use them to buy your employees a goose each for Christmas Day."

"Thank you, miss!"

Matthew carried the packaged articles out to his carriage and handed Trudy up.

"Do you always sling your gold about like the King of Wandara?" Matthew asked in a troubled voice as soon as he had joined her on the seat.

"Oh, it's not mine," she assured him breezily. "I only found it."

He stared at her. "You found it?"

"Yes. You would be surprised, I daresay, to learn how much money people drop."

"Undoubtedly. And you . . . pick it up?"

She nodded, not certain why he was looking at her so strangely. "I am very good at finding gold."

Matthew took a deep, delaying breath. "A useful

talent," was all he said before some other thought took over and he laughed.

The coachman started up the horses.

"May I escort you home?" There was a challenge in his voice.

"No, thank you. I have decided to deliver the gloves right away. There is no reason to wait for Christmas Eve if the men have need of them now."

"A good point. Still, I could wait and take you home."

"I had rather you did not."

"Oh?" His amusement had fled. "Why?"

Trudy could tell that her answer was important to him. It was a matter of trust. Thus far she had prevented him from calling on her, and he wanted to know why.

"Because my house is all at sixes and sevens," she answered truthfully. "As you might imagine, I am rather an indifferent housekeeper, and I would like to set things straight before you call."

"Then I *shall* call?"

His question, uttered in his deepest, quietest voice, made her shiver with anticipation. "Oh, yes." Her words came out in the softest whisper, which seemed to please him, for he gently took her hand.

"Would it offend you," he said, raising her fingers to his lips, "to hear that I find you the most enchanting creature I've ever known?" The warmth of his breath on her fingertips felt like a thermal spring in bitter winter. But to her dismay, his touch seemed more distant than it had when she'd been trapped inside his gloves. It was as if her own magic blocked the deeper thrill of feeling. She wanted that feeling back again, of being one with Matthew.

"No." She shook her head sadly, and she could see she had puzzled him again. Of course she was the most enchanting creature he'd ever known. She was probably the only elf maid he'd ever seen.

"Faye."

She liked the sound of that name upon his lips.

"I don't know how else to say this, but I have an overwhelming desire to kiss you."

"You do?" His confession brought a rush to her cheeks. "But we have no mistletoe."

"Do we need it?"

"I should like you to kiss me under the mistletoe," she said wistfully.

Trudy could sense his urgency, like a tiger crouched beside her. Her own pulse was beating like a hummingbird's wings, but she wanted their first, perhaps their only kiss in this human world to be perfect. And the mistletoe would make it so.

"Very well." He dropped her hand and sat back, but his eyes still gleamed like a cat's in the jungle. "I shall have to wait, but will you promise me that when I ask you again, you will not keep me waiting?"

"Yes," she whispered. She might have made him promise that he would follow her then as well, but she could not bring herself to do that to Matthew. He would see where she was trying to lead, and he would make up his own mind.

Chapter Eight

*T*he time for luring Matthew into the mists—if Trudy was going to do it—was drawing near, for the number of days left before Christmas were few. She only hoped that when the time came she would not experience any qualms, for she'd been burdened with them of late. She knew she wanted Matthew for herself, and the only possible way to keep him was to bring him to live with her in her world. But the thought of tricking him had lost all its appeal. She had seen and felt the misery other people's treachery had brought him. The more she knew him, the more she feared the moment when he would discover what she really was.

If it weren't for this wretched need she felt to tell the truth every time she spoke to him, things would be better, she thought. But the truth was she almost felt as if she were a different creature when she was with him—as if she were Faye.

And she liked being Faye. She liked walking about the streets of Westminster, where the gentlemen tipped their hats to her. She liked going to the park where the nursemaids walked with their charges. She loved hanging on Matthew's arm when he escorted her into shops. She had even enjoyed surprising Mr. Waite with his pair of gloves, for she had never anticipated how endearingly his ears would turn red with pleasure upon receiving them.

But what astonished her most was how her restlessness had vanished. She no longer yearned to wander the globe in search of an elusive thrill. When she walked the world as Faye, she almost felt tied to the ground, and it was not a feeling she despised.

True, her elfin spirit kept her from being rooted to it, the way a human was, and she could not help feeling that something was missing, just as she had felt when her magic had dulled the thrill of Matthew's touch. But all in all, this adventure had meant more to her than any other she had ever had, and she did not want it to end.

How it would end, and when, were questions that loomed before her now. She felt the setting must be perfect. To make certain it was, she stole to the woods outside London one night to recruit a cast and crew for the event.

She found her Aunt Petunia and took her to the fringes of Hyde Park where she thought she might place a house for Matthew to see. It would look a bit strange, standing by itself with its back to the expanse of the park. But she thought she should put her residence off the Kensington Road in the theory that Matthew would never have searched for it there. She could always say it had recently been built. And to confirm that impression, she would make it in the Regency style.

Aunt Petunia, who was draped in a swirling cloak

with silver trim, was all for furnishing the rooms in Louis Quatorze, the style she had most fancied as a child.

"Oh, no no no," Trudy said hastily. "That would be far too grandiose. I don't think Matthew would like it."

"My dear"—Petunia took on a cautioning note— "your young man *is* a gentleman, is he not? You mustn't forget who your family were on your mother's side."

"I have not forgotten, Auntie. And Matthew's lineage is quite good enough. His father was a Scottish baron."

"Ah, he will do then." Petunia's plump face relaxed in soft lines like a bowl of custard. Though at least 185, she was still a pretty elf, but she had begun to wrinkle. "Grace tells me he is handsome enough." She winked. "I've a mind to play your chaperone so I can flirt with him myself."

Trudy sighed and said she might do as she pleased so long as she did nothing to alert Matthew to her plans.

It was in the middle of this conversation that Francis appeared, swimming out of the mists settling over the park.

"So, yer finally getting down to business." He glared at Trudy as if he did not know what to make of her behavior. "What's been taking ye so long?"

"Oh, nothing in particular. But where have you been? I thought you meant to keep an eye on me."

"Aye, but a few o' the fellows got a game up with some trolls over on Hounslow Heath, and I couldn't pass up the chance to beat them pesky creatures."

"You've been gone for the better part of six weeks."

"Is that a fact?" Francis scratched at his beard. "Well, I daresay we might've played more than one match."

"And as far away as Hounslow Heath? My, but haven't you become the traveler, now! I thought you were afraid of such heathenish places. Isn't that where highwaymen hang about?"

"That's very droll, Trudy. I can see that while ye've been flirtin' with humans, ye've been workin' on yer sense of humor. Very droll, indeed."

"Thank you, Francis. Now, if you will just excuse me, I have work to do."

"Work?" Francis scoffed. "Since when did it take any work to lure a feverish man into the mists? Do ye tell me that Sir Matthew's been too sharp for ye, lass?"

"No." With an effort, Trudy hid her misgivings. "But Matthew's fever is nearly cured, and I've been occupied with other matters."

"Like gettin' a bit o' polish?"

His wicked look made her start. "What do you mean?"

"Well, for starters, there's a difference in yer voice. Or haven't ye noticed? It's all hoity-toity-like."

Trudy felt a flush stealing up from her toes. "No, can't say as I have. Do you really find me different?"

"Aye." Francis wrinkled his brow. "Can't say that I like it too much neither. It don't sound natural."

"No? Well, if I want yer opinion, I'll ask for it."

"There." He relaxed with a grin. "Now, that's

more like our Trudy. What've ye planned for Sir Matthew, then?"

"That's for me to know and you to find out," Trudy replied, though she was not so sure she knew herself. She only had a feeling—no, a certainty—that Matthew would be calling for her this week. And if she could get him into her house of illusion, she could lead him from there into the park and off into the mists more easily than if they started anywhere else. But she didn't want Francis hovering over her to see how she would manage it, for he was sure to take exception to her methods.

She was relieved when Aunt Petunia said much the same thing, only with a different tack. "Just you run along now, Francis," she said in that motherly tone older women can get away with. "Trudy and I have our work cut out for us, and we don't need any male help." She giggled. "I haven't had so much fun in ages."

"Yer in good hands, sister." Francis nodded approvingly at their aunt. "If I don't have to worry about ye, I can get back to me game, I guess."

"It's still going then?" Trudy hid her relief.

"I don't mean that one, ye ninny." Francis frowned at her obtuseness. "We've set up a great lot o' games on the heath for the Yule. Ye haven't forgotten the date, now, have ye? Ye'll be there, won't ye?"

"Of course. I couldn't miss Christmas Eve with the family." Though Trudy wondered what Matthew would think of their wild celebration on the heath. Would he think it as savage as the rituals he'd seen in Africa?

She almost blushed for her kind. Then she scolded herself for letting human influence make her ashamed of her own family.

"I'll be there," Trudy said stoutly. "And I'll have Matthew there with me. You'll see."

"If ye don't, I'll come see what's keeping ye," Francis promised with a searching look. It was as if he had seen inside her heart where all her confusion resided.

The thought that he might have guessed her tumult of feelings scared Trudy, though she didn't know why. Perhaps because of the kiss she planned to share with Matthew and the butterflies that fluttered in her stomach at the thought. Or did she fear that his kiss, with the potency of its thrill blocked by her magic, would disappoint her?

Francis took himself off, and Trudy purposely directed her full attention to Aunt Petunia's suggestions for her house.

Matthew was more than just impatient to see Faye again. He feared the wait would make him feverish in spite of the fact that his illness seemed at last to have waned. He had heard of such things occurring. A man brought back from the tropics might experience bouts of fever for a year or years. Then, if he survived the constant weakening and any other disease that might overtake him in the interim, he might begin to see a return to health. Not perfect health, but still he might go on indefinitely without a recurrence of those wretched bouts of ague.

He sensed he had reached that point when he

might never have those fevers again. He should be glad, but as a consequence he would never be visited by his elf friends either. Francis had long since abandoned Matthew's hallucinations as had most of his bad dreams. But Trudy . . .

Matthew thought about Trudy and the almost certain feeling he'd had that the touch of her hands had cured him. Ridiculous, of course. She was nothing more than an illusion derived from his attraction to Faye. He wondered if Faye's hands would feel as magical upon him as Trudy's had, and he suspected they might feel much more so. He could hardly wait to experiment and see, but he could do nothing until she allowed him.

And such activities meant marriage. In the past few days, Matthew had come to the realization that that was what he wanted. Faye, with her intelligence and spirit, her courage and her beauty, would be a better wife than he could possibly ask for. But would she want him? A man whom many considered fit for the grave? He wouldn't die now; he was certain. But neither could he claim to be the strong young man he'd once been. Faye seemed so young, but his unnatural aging had not seemed to disturb her. More than once she'd pooh-poohed his attempts to draw that distinction between them. He'd hoped it was because she still found him attractive despite his weakness and his scars, but perhaps he had read far too much into her replies.

"Saab?" Ahmad entered his library. "A note has come for you."

Matthew resisted the temptation to grab it. He

hoped it was from Faye and would give him permission to call.

But as soon as he saw the engraved words, he felt a wave of disappointment.

"An invitation," he said to Ahmad in a contemplative tone, "and to a Christmas ball from one of the members of the Association committee. Well, it's clear that I must have been forgiven. It's been years since anyone's invited me to anything."

"That is good, saab. It is good to take your place in society, yes?"

"Better than I care to admit. When I was younger, I put no value on such things. But . . ." Matthew hesitated before going on. He raised his eyes to his loyal friend's. Ahmad had the right to know what was in his mind.

Ahmad's return stare convinced him that he had sensed Matthew had something serious to impart. "Yes, Matthew saab?"

"I was about to say that when a gentleman contemplates marriage, he begins to care more about his place in society. For his wife's sake, of course."

Ahmad betrayed no surprise. His demeanor was sober, rather than overjoyed. "Did you not consider being married before, Matthew saab? To Helen memsaab?"

"Yes, I did." Matthew felt all the embarrassment of that error. He had not truly loved Helen. He saw that now. "You are trying to say that I had no such consideration of her, which is true. I hope to choose more wisely this time."

"To choose Faye Meriwether, is this not so?" Ahmad was troubled. "You believe she has helped you win the support of your colleagues again. Is that it, saab?"

"Whether I believe she did or not is not the issue. I must have her, Ahmad. It is that simple." As Matthew had held her hand in his carriage, he had discovered this to be true.

"Then in that case, Matthew saab, I hope you shall have her." Enigmatically Ahmad added, "And I shall do my best to see she does not escape."

Matthew grinned. "I hesitate to ask what you mean, but I hope you're not suggesting that I'm incapable of conducting my own love affairs. I assure you I am well practiced with women."

"No, saab." Ahmad allowed himself a smile. "I have great faith in the famous Matthew saab when it comes to pleasing ladies. You forget, but I have seen you charm more than one princess from the arms of her prince."

"All those instances are best forgotten," Matthew said, firmly pushing such memories into the past. He hoped that Faye would forgive him for his past transgressions—circumstances being what they'd been—but just to insure she would, he would not mention them. His lady love possessed an open mind, but he would not strain its boundaries with useless confessions.

After Ahmad had retired, Matthew studied the invitation in his hand. The ball was to be on Christmas Eve, which was only a few days away. Faye had promised to kiss him under the mistletoe.

Well, it appeared that fate had provided them with a golden opportunity. Matthew now had a tool and a date with which to force her hand.

He took up his quill and ink to write two missives: one to his hosts to beg another card for the ball for a lady friend, the other to solicit Faye's company for the evening. When he had finished the latter, his sense of anticipation was as high as it had ever been—far higher than when he had set off on his conquests. That a woman should make him feel as if to win her would be greater than all other possible glory made him wonder whether he might not be feverish again.

But when much later that night Trudy awakened him with a whisper, he did not feel achy at all. His thoughts were clear, and his dreams had been free of all horror. All his senses went on alert. The sound of her voice sent ripples through him like the wind over water. Her fresh-flower scent drifted through the air to tickle his nostrils. And when he saw her poised for flight at the foot of his bed, he felt as if his vision had been blessed with the sight of such celestial beauty as to make the perfect recollection of it impossible.

Her mere presence in his bedroom had aroused him. The sight of her exotic face with its pale green eyes and the ears that peaked beside it so charmingly gave him a rush of desire such as he'd never known. He decided that a dream must have conjured her this time instead of a hallucination, his feelings were so intense.

Trudy seemed to sense that his capacities as well were undiminished by chills, for she remained a safe distance away from his far-reaching arms. If she had not, Matthew knew he might have tried to staunch his need by grabbing her in the next instant.

As it was, however, he was afraid to move for fear of chasing her away. He had not expected another visit from Trudy. His dream maiden occupied a special place in his heart, one he was likely to lose at any moment. And he could not help wondering, if Faye became his wife, how near the reality of marriage would come to the perfection of his nighttime visits from Trudy.

Would Faye have the ability to cure him with a touch of her hand? Could she soothe him with her magical voice? Would she be willing to come to him in the night to vanquish all his haunting memories?

"Hullo, mannie," Trudy said, and his heart melted with the sound of her familiar voice.

"Hullo, Trudy. I had not looked for you tonight."

"I know. I thought I'd come around just to see how you were doing before I go off with my family to celebrate the Yule."

"Tell me about your celebration, Trudy."

"Would you like to hear about it?" Her voice sounded almost wistful, as if some expected sadness had burdened it.

"Yes, I'd like to hear about that and other things that only you could tell me."

"Such as?"

It was foolish, and yet he thought she could tell him. As if by some magic, his own mind could leave the limitations of his body and float to places that body could no longer take him. "Such as . . . tell me about the White River of the Nile, Trudy. I came so close to its source. I could almost feel it. . . ."

She approached him now, gliding noiselessly over his coverlets, and Matthew felt her fingertips closing his eyelids, soothing him, drawing pictures out of the darkness before his eyes, pictures of the fog-shrouded Mountains of the Moon.

"I'll show you, mannie," she whispered, and her voice was Faye's voice. The similarity sent chill after chill down his spine. "If you would come with me, mannie, I could show you everything."

"I don't need to see everything. Just tell me about the Nile."

She sighed, and he thought she might refuse. But then her palms slowly covered his face, making his vision that much larger. "Can you see them, mannie? The Mountains of the Moon?"

"Yes, I see them." To his surprise, the fog had lifted from them, and he saw that their peaks were covered with ice and snow. The significance of those long-hidden glaciers did not escape him. "So the river does come from here?"

"Yes, it does. But it's far more complicated than that. Are you with me?"

"Yes." He sensed that they were going on a tumultuous journey, so he grasped her wrists to hold on.

Trudy gave a gasp. But Matthew kept his hold so gentle and so unthreatening, she finally relaxed. The Mountains of the Moon came back into focus in all their snowy splendor.

"Then what, Trudy?" Matthew asked in his best taming voice, sensing that he'd scared her but unwilling to let her go. Her touch was more than exquisite. It was an intimate and sensuous entry into another world.

"Can you see the streams, Matthew?"

And he could, so he nodded. And his lips brushed her palms.

Her hands gave a tremble.

"Yes, I see them." He kissed her palms lightly to calm her.

Trudy's face, Faye's face, was floating above his vision of the mountain's icy streams. Matthew had never seen an image so beautiful.

"You'd better stop that now or you'll miss the rest."

"The temptation is overwhelming."

"Yer telling me."

He chuckled. Now she was his Trudy again. "Very well. I shall promise to behave if you'll show me the rest."

She sighed, more deeply this time, and he fancied her a bit disappointed, but—he would oblige her later.

And oblige himself.

"The streams," she continued in a dreamier voice, "all run downhill until they empty into a vast *nyanza*, or lake, as you Britishers call it."

"I can see it," Matthew said. Its waters had spread in her palms like a plate of glass.

"Do you see the bay at its northern end?"

Matthew wanted to nod, but he felt a need to hold on, for he was rushing then, rushing with the pent-up waters of the lake toward a high ridge that loomed suddenly in his vision.

"Do you see the break?"

He not only saw it. He felt his body falling through the enormous gap in the rock, falling down and down some sixteen feet, while the start of the fierce white river surged with him.

Then he was swept down the gorge where great white cliffs towered hundreds of feet above him, forcing all that snowy water into a narrow, jumping ribbon of foam. Matthew clenched his teeth, reining back a shout of pure exhilaration.

No wonder no European had found it, the source of the mysterious White River, for it was hidden in this gorge, which no man could risk upon danger of death. Yet he was seeing it here, in his bedroom, and no matter how impossible, no matter if it had come to him in a dream, Matthew knew it was real.

His mind, for all its English schooling in logic and science, had been exposed to hundreds of other ways and other beliefs. He believed that whatever Trudy was, a dream or an illusion or the elf she called herself, she had shown him what he needed to make all his travels complete. And it did not matter that he couldn't make these discoveries known or claim them for himself. It only mattered that he'd seen this before he died.

His wild river ride had glided to a pause as the waters fell to the plains, where they spread in a marsh in all directions, like a pitcher of cream that's been poured into a bowl. Under the surface, where no one could see them, slow-moving currents secretly carried them north to the sea. Other streams mixed with Matthew's stream to make it stronger. The water had to travel many more miles before he would be able to recognize it as the White River he had known, but he had seen enough to satisfy him.

Slowly, gently, Matthew removed his hands from Trudy's and allowed her to lift her palms from his face.

"Did you see all you wanted to see, mannie?" Her green eyes glowed in the darkness of his room once again.

"Yes, thank you, Trudy. It was everything and more than I'd imagined. That was a lovely Yule gift."

"Do you mind so much not being there?"

"No. As glorious as it was, I'd far rather be here with you."

Matthew paused. All his desire flooded back in an instant. If she was only a dream, then he could indulge his deepest wants. He shouldn't have to bear with his powerful need any longer. "Will you come lie with me, Trudy?" he asked.

She extended a hand, which he tried to take, but at the same time she floated backward out of his reach. "I can't come to you yet, mannie. Not like this."

"Like what, then?"

But her voice began to fade, and it seemed she dragged the back of one hand over her eyes. "We'll have to wait until we're both in the same world for it to be right."

"Yes." He thought he knew what his dream was trying to tell him. It was Faye he should be pursuing, not his phantom figure, no matter how much he loved her.

"Then I shan't be seeing you anymore," he said.

She looked startled, even fearful. "Yes, you will. You'll be seeing me sooner than you think."

And in a blink, she was gone. Matthew lay awake, wondering if he had come to consciousness just as rapidly as she had disappeared. But his throat was all clogged with need, and the delicate scent of her still lingered in the air.

The gift she had given him was still clear in his mind, his wild river ride, the secret of the source. After such a beautiful dream, he ought to have felt soothed. But instead he was troubled.

Chapter Nine

$\mathcal{T}$rudy was troubled, too.

She had been hiding behind the door to Matthew's library when he had told Ahmad of his intentions, and she had suffered a great shock. Even she, an elf, knew that his affair with Faye was progressing much more rapidly than convention dictated, but she had never imagined he would think of marriage—and so soon.

She ought to have known that a man of Matthew's quick impulses and determined mind would not tarry over any decision, even a matter of the heart. He had decided that he wanted Faye, and that was that. He would never stop to consider how few times he had actually seen her or even who she really was. Of course, if one counted the nighttime visits from Trudy, he'd spoken with her twice as often as he realized, but Trudy could not tell whether those visits had played any part in his decision.

She felt a certain intimacy with Matthew at night when he allowed himself to confide his secrets to her, an entirely different sort by day when he supposed her to be human. But never once since they had first met did she feel the way she had expected to feel—like a superior being who was toying with a pet of challenging intelligence.

Oh, Matthew was a challenge all right. Yet Trudy knew, despite all the claims she'd made to the contrary, that she would never be able to lead Matthew around by the nose.

Not unless he followed her into the mists, where she could confuse him so terribly, he would be grateful to submit to her will. The thought of Matthew tamed and on his knees, however, brought her no sense of triumph at all. It made her miserable. With a feeling of dread, she thought she knew why, but that was a thought she could not admit, even to herself.

She intercepted Matthew's invitation by blowing it out of his messenger's hands over a fence and into a private garden. She had allowed the boy to search for Meadows Lane just long enough to feel a merited frustration but not nearly long enough for him to determine that a street by that name did not exist. Trudy was sufficiently familiar with human foibles to suspect that he would be unlikely to report his failure to deliver the note. She followed him a ways just to make certain. But after giving a weary shrug, he skipped off in the opposite direction from Matthew's lodgings.

Tut-tutting over this irresponsible behavior, which was deplorably unworthy of anyone with a soul, Trudy clutched Matthew's missive to her chest and climbed up into a tree. She read it there, lingering over his every word.

He would be *delighted*, he said, and *honored* if she

would agree to accompany him to a ball on Christmas Eve. The words were conventional, she knew. Yet with a shivering thrill Trudy could imagine all Matthew's feelings behind them. She did not have to wonder whether he recalled her request about the mistletoe, for Matthew had appended a postscript reminding her of her promise.

Christmas dances were notoriously liberal in one respect. Mistletoe was sure to be hung somewhere from the ceiling to catch the unwary, and a gentleman would be forgiven any liberties he might take when under the influence of the "healing" weed.

In her excitement over the prospect of her first human ball, Trudy almost forgot about her own family's Christmas ritual. Then with a pang she remembered she had promised Francis she would come to the heath. And with Matthew in thrall.

The thought of that other celebration brought none of the excitement that Matthew's invitation did. With a feeling almost like the recollection of a nightmare, she recalled all her previous Christmas Eves.

The witches and trolls came to the heath, riding their wolves, brooms, or shovels to the gathering place, where they danced riotously under stones. The air was always full of noise, the music of lyres and flutes, the shouts from dancing and drinking. A great fire was always lit to protect them from the Reaper, who roamed the hills on Christmas Eve. The animals spoke to their friends at midnight. And the water of the streams turned to wine.

Trudy recalled how lonely she had always felt on Christmas Eve, realizing now that she never felt lonely with Matthew. If only he would come with her, perhaps she could learn to enjoy the elfin revelries at last.

But whether he came or not, she thought with a rare misgiving, she had every intention of enjoying herself at her first Christmas ball.

She wrapped her cloak about her and created another outfit in which to go shopping. She had to have something new and splendid to wear to the ball, but all the patterns she had already copied were for less formal attire. With one last look at Matthew's invitation, one last brush of her fingertips over his bold handwriting, she tucked the paper into her stylish reticule. She wasn't sure just where she could keep his note. As a rule elves did not weigh themselves down with keepsakes; they hoarded nothing but gold. Trudy knew, however, that nothing would part her from this precious souvenir, even if she had to wear it always beneath her clothes.

Climbing down from her tree, she walked the several blocks to Bond Street, protected by her cloak. If any man chose to bother her, all she had to do was make herself invisible with one sweep of it about her shoulders. This, she'd discovered, was far more effective than haughty looks. Feeling rather melancholy this morning, she was determined to enjoy the evidence of the season, so she meandered on her way.

The doors of many aristocrats' houses had their knockers removed, which showed that the families had retired to the country for the season. But London was full of people with no country residence and with single gentlemen and ladies such as herself. One had only to look around to see their preparations for Christmas Eve.

There was a bustle in the streets. Grocers were sending raisins and currants to their customers for their Christmas puddings. Serving men delivered geese and ribs of beef, while scullery maids, working behind the dwellings, scoured cooking pots. The smell of chestnuts roasting over flames wafted from the braziers set up on every corner, and the freshness of evergreens and fruit scented the air.

Chandlers were busy delivering large molded candles to the houses in Berkeley Square, and the coopers' wagons were weighted down with Yule logs for any house whose fireplace would hold them.

Trudy saw all this, and her heart filled with anxious anticipation of her first Christmas Eve with Matthew. She hoped it would not be her last.

The elegant modiste in the shop she'd frequented in Bond Street cautioned Trudy that it would be difficult to engage a seamstress at this late date. Anyone who was talented enough to make a gown on the order of what she'd described would be completely taken up with previous orders. The modiste suggested that Trudy take a look at a ready-made gown she said was certain to please her.

Trudy had intended to purchase another pattern to make her own dress, but the flash of green velvet caught her eye. The modiste held the high-waisted gown up before her in front of the mirror, and from the woman's rapturous sigh, Trudy was reassured that the image she saw in the glass was all she perceived it to be.

The gown's shade of green altered with the light, the way the color of forest leaves changes with the angle of the sun's rays, making her eyes one moment as dark as summer ivy, the next as light as a winter sea. Trudy's cheeks glowed with their customary roses, but their pink had been enhanced by her walk and the anticipation of Matthew's kiss. Her black hair sparkled even by the poor shop light. Trudy decided she could do nothing better than to copy this dress, but to be fair to the modiste, she bought it. The woman thought it rather odd that she would not try it on, but the mere thought of doing so made Trudy shake with an unreasoning fear.

Most elves refused even to touch human clothes. The surest way to rid oneself of a nighttime visitor was to offer him or her a gift of a garment. Trudy was not so superstitious as to fear touching human garments; still, the lessons of a lifetime made gooseflesh travel down her back when the shopkeeper pressed her to try on the gown. Trudy was obliged to assume a haughty air to shut the woman up, but she could see in the end that the shopkeeper's motives had been innocent. She'd simply wanted to see how her favorite creation would look on a creature as divinely lovely as Faye.

Armed with her dress wrapped up in a parcel, Trudy stepped out of the shop and started to make her way home. If "home" was what she should consider it, she mused. It was long past time to conjure her house, if for no other reason than at least to have a better mirror than the reflection offered her by the Serpentine or the Thames.

She flew to the park, and in the space she'd selected, drew up the illusion of her house. When she'd finished, an elegant residence both strongly built and in the Regency style stood at the end of a short lane, surrounded by trees. Trudy left off all her Aunt Petunia's suggestions for embellishments in order to maintain the simplicity she thought Matthew would prefer.

Making a key, she unlocked the bolt and went upstairs. Once alone in her own room—which Matthew would never see but which she perversely fitted out just to suit her mood—she held the gown up in front of her again. The urge to put it on was almost more than she could resist, but she knew she must not.

She wondered sadly how her whole body would feel with her magic suspended. She asked herself how long it would take her to adjust to living without it. More than anything she wanted to know if the thrill of Matthew's kiss would be magnified if she wore the gown.

With an anxious feeling—which made her wonder why she was asking such foolish questions—she had to admit to herself that it would. Just as she had already felt in that brief instant when their hands had touched inside her glove.

Would she ever again experience such a thrill? What would it be worth giving up to make certain that she did? And more important, would she want to go on living if she could not?

Now, there ye have it. That's how our Trudy got herself in such a deep pickle by Christmas Eve. And I'll admit that I should've been watchin' her instead of playin' with them trolls. But how was I to know what sort o' nonsense a sensible elf like Trudy would get up to when a fellow wasn't around? So ye can't really say it was me fault.

By this time, o' course, I could see that Trudy was up to some strange kind o' mischief, so all the while she was aprimpin' in front of her mirror, I was awatchin' her from a tree. I could see that somethin' was botherin' her, somethin' more than just a toothache, which is the worst sort o' pain I've ever felt. But I couldn't quite tell what it was, ye see? That's because it was her conscience, which is a thing I don't have and don't need. For a conscience is a troublesome thing to an elf, which is why we don't bother ourselves to get them.

But I had this eerie feeling like, as if somethin' bad were goin' to happen. Only I didn't know exactly what because, as ye've seen, Trudy didn't really know herself. All I knew was I had better stick around in case somethin' went wrong with them plans of hers, 'cause I could see she was getting in deeper than she ought.

And why she would want to play with a dangerous thing like that dress, as if she couldn't make anything she wanted of her own . . .

So, ye'll say I should've seen the trouble coming, but I did not, and so this was how it happened. . . .

On the night of the ball, Matthew found Ahmad waiting for him downstairs in the corridor. The

Pathan's thick, black brows rose in an arch at the sight of Matthew's elegant garb as he descended the stairs.

Ahmad gave a deep salaam. "You are looking very well this evening, Matthew saab."

"Thank you, Ahmad." Matthew brushed his fingers over his evening clothes: a new black jacket, a white brocaded waistcoat, and a pair of tight-fitting black satin breeches with hose to match. "Not too much like a scarecrow, I hope."

"No, saab. It seems you have recovered your weight."

"Not entirely. But the difference is no more than a good tailor can hide."

"You will be calling for Miss Meriwether, saab?"

"That is right." Matthew pulled the note she had sent today from his pocket. "I have the directions to her house. I confess it is not an area I am familiar with." Matthew handed Ahmad the piece of paper, which, as was Faye's custom, had been printed in gold. The fact that she'd bothered with such an expense in this particular instance troubled him more than he liked to say.

But Ahmad made no reference to the gold lettering as he frowned at the note. "The last time I rode on that side of the park, I do not recall seeing a street by that name."

"She tells me her lane is quite new. Part of one of these new developments."

"Ah, that will explain it, saab."

Ahmad's voice did not sound as convinced as his words implied, but Matthew let the subject drop. He took the note and placed it deep inside his pocket.

"And what will you do this evening? Visit the almshouse again?" Ahmad had made a practice of visiting the inmates quite often to play at chess.

"No, I shall take a walk." Ahmad's glance was casual as he asked, "If you do not mind, I shall ride with you as far as Miss Meriwether's house. The night is fine for a walk in the park."

"Of course I don't mind. But you will beware of footpads, won't you?"

Ahmad grinned and patted his belt where Matthew knew he concealed a large knife inside his baggy trousers.

"No need to worry, saab. Your park holds no terrors for me."

"I should say not. Not compared to those frightful mountains of yours. Still, it's as well not to become too complacent. Danger is danger, no matter how tame in comparison."

Ahmad nodded, and his expression was more serious than the occasion seemed to warrant. "I agree. May I suggest, saab, that you keep on your guard as well?"

"Me? At a ball?" Matthew scoffed. "You must be thinking that I shall trip while I'm dancing, but I assure you my friend, our English dances are so lacking in violence that I shall have no opportunity to wound myself."

"As you say, saab. All the same I urge you to be cautious. Things are not always what they seem."

Matthew chose to ignore Ahmad's true meaning. He knew his friend still had reservations about Faye. But in spite of her mysterious ways, Matthew had made up his mind.

"Yes," he answered, deflecting Ahmad's comment. "We have both discovered that in the past few days." He smiled. "Helen is not quite the faithless woman I thought her. And Julian—though still a prig—was no more a traitor to me than I was to him."

As he'd expected, Ahmad was diverted by this speech. "He has still dishonored your name. In my country a man would seek revenge for his insults."

"And the feuds would rage back and forth until no member of his family was left. No, Ahmad"—Matthew shrugged himself into his greatcoat—"I think this is one thing my culture has mastered better than yours: forgiveness." He grinned. "You should practice it. It makes life so much more pleasant."

"But I have been practicing forgiveness, Matthew saab," Ahmad said as he helped Matthew into his sleeves. "If I had not, you would have been knifed in your bed for all the curses you have flung at me."

"Touché." Matthew winced. "Although I am not sure one can call it forgiveness when you take revenge by constantly reminding me of my rudeness to you."

Ahmad's smile contained a wealth of magnanimity. "Sir Matthew was not himself."

Matthew was happy to see that Ahmad's good humor had been restored. He did not want his Pathan friend to worry about Faye and what she might be. To Matthew her origins were immaterial. He had seen enough death to know that life was short and not to be wasted on foolish considerations such as birth or position. If Faye's father had been a wealthy cit, she possessed more than enough charm and poise to overcome that stigma. If she was a thief, he could only approve her particular brand of roguery. And if—as he more than half suspected—she was merely an enchanting kind of eccentric, he was eccentric enough himself to keep up with her.

Matthew looked at his friend more seriously. "There have been many times," he said, "when I have not been myself. But do you know, Ahmad, I think I have never felt more at peace than I do right now."

Instead of the comfort he had hoped his words would bring, a new consternation arose in Ahmad's eyes. But Matthew's friend did not give voice to it.

Instead, he said, "I should wish you a merry Christmas, saab, for I do not expect I shall see you before morning."

"Thank you, Ahmad. Shall we go?"

Chapter Ten

The streets of Westminster that Christmas Eve were thickly crowded with all sorts of conveyances. At the last moment Matthew had been obliged to bribe a driver in order to secure a carriage. He might more easily have hired a couple of chairs, but he refused to give up this chance of privacy with Faye. The question he had to pose her was best left until the end of the evening, and he would be damned if he'd propose marriage out in the street. Since he was not at all certain he would be invited into her house after the ball, he decided the carriage would be a necessity.

This driver as well claimed no knowledge of Meadows Lane, but Matthew assured him the street had only recently been built, so the man followed his directions. As soon as the lane appeared—short and possessed of only one house at the end—Ahmad begged to be set down.

"I shall see you at breakfast." Matthew tossed off the remark, his eyes already fixed on the doorway ahead. It gleamed as white as sunlight in the black of the night, like a brilliant beacon in the fog.

"Take care, Matthew saab." Ahmad's words seemed

to echo behind him in the quiet street as the hired chaise rolled on to its destination.

No other houses had been built on the lane as yet, although graceful lamps had been spaced along its length. As the horses neared the end, the structure that greeted Matthew's eyes was so new and fresh that no soot had sullied its bricks. Its eaves were shining with white paint. Its windows sparkled with an unnatural cleanliness, while with the exception of an occasional evergreen, all around it the trees of the park loomed in leafless silence. A clump or two of mistletoe, which must have escaped the Christmas revelers, hugged their empty limbs. As Matthew stepped down, the wind seemed to ruffle them, as if they bent to see him.

With his mind on mistletoe and the pleasures it would bring, Matthew abandoned his quick examination of the house and strode up onto the porch. He had barely pulled the bell when the door was thrown open by a footman, who grinned at Matthew in a most unseemly manner.

Taking the servant's good humor as evidence of some celebration going on belowstairs, Matthew wished him joy of the season and identified himself. The footman asked Matthew to follow him into a nearby parlor where he might wait.

All the furniture inside seemed as new as the outside of the house, although its style was more masculine and comfortable. Not having known what to expect, Matthew was reassured by Faye's good taste, which seemed so perfectly to suit his own. He only wondered that she should have considered her household to be in disarray when it was plainly in excellent order with the exception of that one servant's demeanor. He decided that despite Faye's protestations, she must be a far more exacting housekeeper than she'd allowed.

Before this contradiction could raise other questions in his mind, he was distracted by the entrance of a plump, tiny lady, draped in lavender satin. She swept into the room with a flourish, made him an elaborate curtsy, and extended one dainty hand for him to kiss.

"Sir Matthew Dunstone?" she inquired with a downward sweep of black lashes over violet eyes.

Matthew had never had the patience to be a gallant, but something about this pretty woman, who reminded him of Faye, made him pleased to extend her the courtesy. He bowed low over her hand and let his lips brush her fingers, which he found to be as soft as rose petals and strongly scented with lilac. "Ma'am? I am afraid you have the advantage over me."

She giggled, and the roses in her cheeks bloomed. To Matthew's astonishment, they seemed the result of purest nature rather than rouge.

"I am Faye's Aunt Petunia," she said. "She has asked me to bear you company while she puts the finishing touches on her toilette. I hope you do not mind," she added with a daring wink.

Her flirtatious manner obliged Matthew to respond in kind. "Your question puts me at a disadvantage once again. I cannot say that I mind without being untruthful, nor can I own to being delighted for fear of giving offense to your niece."

This remark seemed to tickle her enormously.

She took a delicate Japanese fan—a trinket he had not noticed her wearing—raised it to her lips, then tapped his wrist with it.

"Lud! But you are a naughty boy," she said in a style reminiscent of the previous century. "And I shall have to caution my niece to have a look to you."

At her statement a new concern arose in Matthew. He had been counting upon the expectation that he and Faye would be alone, but her aunt's unanticipated presence suggested otherwise.

"Are you to accompany us to the ball, madam?" he asked in a tone that was as polite as he could muster.

"Heavens, no!" Faye's Aunt Petunia laughed and touched one hand to her dimpled cheek. "Why, Faye would have my head upon a platter if I did! Although I should dearly love to dance with you, young man. And perhaps I shall, one of these fine, dewy evenings."

Even Matthew, with his wealth of experience, was startled by such a bold remark. Eccentricity seemed to run in Faye's family—if not total madness. He was beginning to think he understood the reason for Faye's avoidance of polite society, for it would be difficult for such a free spirit to drift where she wanted in a pond thick with sharks who might wish to make an issue over slight differences in comportment.

But for all her eccentricity, Aunt Petunia seemed to be a lady, at least, and a delightful, though surprising one.

Before he could ask her by what name he should

address her, a rather breathless Faye entered the room. Matthew turned to greet her, and his heart caught in his throat.

Everything about her seemed to sparkle. Her emerald eyes were lit with the softest glow he had ever seen in them. Her welcoming smile was a bright snowy white. Even her hair, which was as soft and as black as midnight, shone as if the moon had lit it. The green dress she wore, which draped her slender figure to the ankles, spoke of holly and mistletoe, and the roses in her cheeks whispered of firelight and kisses. Matthew was struck speechless, as if he were seeing her for the first time.

I *am* besotted, he thought.

Faye, in turn, took in his black evening garb, and he noted her approval of the extra pains he had taken with his appearance tonight.

Her frank admiration, which seemed a hunger to match his own, made his own eyes mist over. Then through that hazy mist he spied something else—a pair of pointed ears nestled in the sharp black of her hair. Green felt for her clothes instead of velvet.

The plaster walls of the room seemed to fade away, letting ghostly trees emerge from the park—

Matthew closed his eyes and pinched the bridge of his nose.

"Matthew?" Faye's voice came close. He felt the soft touch of kid on his cheeks and forehead. "Are you all right?"

He shook his head and opened his eyes, and she was there again as she had been, dressed in green velvet for the ball. The softness of her features soothed him.

"A momentary dizziness," he said, taking a deep appreciative breath. Her scent, a mixture of hedge-rows and lavender, filled his nostrils. "For an instant I feared a return of my fever."

Faye placed the back of her wrist against his brow. "I don't feel any fever," she said, but her face was troubled.

"It's over now." Matthew held her away, then took her gloved hands in his. "I see you've worn my gift."

A rapid flush, greater than anything his remark had warranted, tinged her features. "Yes, I have," she whispered, as if it were a secret to guard between them.

"What is this? What did you say?" Aunt Petunia said sharply from behind him.

"Nothing, Auntie." Faye winked at Matthew. "I am certain you misunderstood." She reached for a handsome cloak that had been thrown upon a chair. Of a sudden, Faye seemed in great haste to be gone. "Sir Matthew just made me a compliment. There is nothing for you to be concerned about."

Faye tugged at his sleeve. Nothing loath—for, in truth, Matthew still felt a bit dizzy—he followed her lead and made his good-byes to her aunt.

"But—did he not say—" she stammered.

Aunt Petunia's pretty face had puckered in concern. For what, he did not know. But it was clear to Matthew that, whatever the cause, it was something Faye did not wish to discuss.

"Have no fears," she called back to her aunt from the front door. "I am in complete control." This last was uttered almost defiantly as she slammed the door.

Matthew's lips began to tickle him. Now that they were out in the street, his vertigo seemed to have cleared, although a dense fog had moved in from the park. As he accompanied Faye down the short walk, he glanced back and saw that mist had completely shrouded the house.

He would have remarked upon the sudden phenomenon, but Faye's earlier comment could not go ignored. "In complete control?" he asked as they reached the carriage. "Dare I beg an explanation?"

"You may beg one if you like." She flashed him a teasing smile.

"But you will choose not to answer, is that it?"

When she nodded, half mischievously, half regretfully, he only chuckled, then waited until they both were seated inside before he said, "Which would deal my masculine vanity a severe blow. Very well, then, I shall not ask. Only tell me that you have nothing cruel in mind, fair lady, for my heart is of no mind to be wounded this evening." He had tried to say this lightly, but it had come out more seriously than he'd intended.

Faye's response, too, was much more sober than he had expected. Dismay clouded her eyes when she said, "No, not cruel. I promise. Whatever the evening holds, I shall not be cruel. You have my word."

Disturbed and even a bit frightened by the distress in her voice, Matthew tried to change the subject. "I was afraid for one terrible moment—no matter how charming your aunt is, mind—that you had planned for her to accompany us."

"No, I told you I lived alone."

"Is she merely visiting, then?"

"Yes, she'll be gone by morning."

Such a blithe dismissal surprised him. But it was all part and parcel of Faye, and what made her unique. "What does she think, I wonder, of your going out tonight without a chaperon?"

"I believe she envies me."

This was said in such a soft, husky voice as to set his blood afire. Wishing he could see her, Matthew reached for her hand in the dark and, when he found it, heard her gasp.

The sound was as virginal as it was eager. It cautioned him to wait. Whatever rules of society Faye had breached, her unguarded reaction to his touch had proven her innocence in this particular regard. And the knowledge that he might be her first and only love gave Matthew an unexpected rush of triumph, so strong, in fact, that his hands began to shake.

Astonished, for he had not thought such a matter important to him, he had trouble finding his tongue. When he did, he used it to divert himself from the temptation churning his blood.

"Would you like to know something about our hosts?" he asked lightly.

"Why, yes. I suppose I should have asked who they are."

He chuckled and drew her hand onto his knee, noticing with pleasure that it trembled just like his. "Our esteemed hosts are Gerald Fortescue, Esquire, and his wife, Lady Patricia, the daughter of the Earl of Albion, both patrons of the African Association. Fortescue is one of the wealthiest men in

Britain, but he prefers town to country, which is the reason you find him still in London. He's both a scholar and an amateur scientist, and his wife shares his passion for the unknown. He's rather a decent sort, and his wife is no less, although some of her friends necessarily lack her level of discernment. I'm afraid you will find both sorts at this function, but it should be more amusing than your typical society affair. Else I would not have bored you with it."

He sensed a hesitation before she said, "You could not have bored me with such an invitation. I—"

"You—?" he prompted, when it appeared she would not continue.

Faye laughed, a musical laugh that made his spirit soar, and Matthew knew he had overcome whatever fear had held him back from loving her.

"I," she said, placing an emphasis on the word, "cannot wait to see a ballroom decked out in Christmas greens."

It was not what she had been about to say, he was sure, but the words reminded him of mistletoe again. And he could only hope she'd been thinking of her promise when she'd spoken.

The carriage came to a jerking stop.

"It appears that we are already here." Matthew opened the door to step down first. Then he turned and helped her to alight, putting his hands upon her tiny waist, which gave him the chance to bring her close and to sniff her hair. She felt weightless, as light as a butterfly.

"I shall endeavor," he whispered into her hair, "to see that the journey home passes much more slowly."

This declaration caused Trudy's pulse to leap as she took Matthew's arm to be escorted in. Fear and exultation seemed to mix equally inside her as she gazed at his profile. Matthew's back was perfectly erect. The cut of his black jacket closely hugged his square shoulders. The strong features of his face and his imposing brow gave him the look of an eagle.

Beside him, Trudy's step was effortlessly light as always; however, when they entered the door, she almost tripped, alarmed by the crush of humans.

One glance at the scene inside told her she was by far the frailest creature present. The men's voices were raised in raucous shouts; the ladies' laughter nearly pierced her ears. Children, as tall as she, chased each other back and forth across the corridor through the crowd. A Christmas ball was not at all the decorous event she had expected, and for one instant she was tempted to draw her cloak about her and simply disappear.

Then Matthew stepped around in front of her, his body shielding her from the noise. He put one finger under her chin to raise her eyes to his.

He did not bother to shout over the din but instead arched one brow as if to ask if they should go in. A sympathetic grin turned up the corners of his lips.

At that moment Trudy heard music from the orchestra, and the prospect of a dance chased her fears away. She had nothing to fear as long as Matthew was beside her.

She took a bracing breath and nodded, giving his elbow a squeeze.

"I'll present you to our hosts," she heard Matthew say as he turned to lead her toward the ballroom.

Nearly lost in a sea of humans, for Matthew's tall back blocked her view, Trudy was surprised when he moved aside to let her precede him through the doorway. A vista opened, and she gasped in delight at the sight of the kissing bough.

It was enormous: Two great rings of holly and ivy were suspended from the ceiling, with sprigs of other evergreens thrown in; shiny red apples dangled cheek by jowl with pale paper roses; colored ribbons, the ends of which had been tied to dolls, and sparkling ornaments made a shimmering fairy forest. The bough hovered over the dancers, who seemed to be wrestling and laughing at the same time. Astonished at first by this behavior, Trudy quickly realized that the gentlemen were attempting to steer their partners under the mistletoe, which hung from a ribbon in the center of the bough, while the ladies were using all their wiles to dodge it.

"Oh, Matthew," she breathed, forgetting to dim her bewitching beauty in her excitement. "It is all so thrilling."

Her smile fell upon the room, and all movement ceased. Even Matthew came to a halt at her side, seeming to freeze under her inadvertent spell. The dancers' music had stopped in the middle of the dance, and they'd all turned to stare.

On the faces of the motionless men she saw an astonishment no less admiring than it was dazed. On the ladies', a mixture of reluctant acknowledgment and dismay had been fixed. With a stunning blow Trudy knew that she did not belong here, that her presence could ruin all the other guests' enjoyment unless she did something immediately to correct her lapse.

With a sweep of her magic cloak, she broke the spell she'd so unwittingly cast upon the guests. She lowered her eyes and with a powerful intake of breath reined her beauty in. In the next instant the first persons to awake from the spell began to stir; then the rest followed as if they'd just remembered where they were. They were still staring at her, but all unnatural amazement had fled.

"Well—" At Trudy's side Matthew spoke while shaking his head with a mild look of annoyance. "I should say our entry was well timed."

"Oh?" she asked breathlessly.

"Yes. I see the music has stopped, and the voices are, therefore, not quite so loud. That should give us a chance to pay our respects."

He swept one hand toward the receiving line to his right. While some conversation had resumed, Trudy knew that most people's eyes were still upon her. She could only hope they would forget the momentary numbness that had struck them all.

Their hosts, however, were waiting to greet her as Matthew presented her, first to Fortescue and then to his wife. Although they seemed reserved at first—a mood left over from their bedazzlement, no doubt—both did their best to make Trudy feel welcome. Gerald Fortescue, a congenial man of slight build, peered deeply into her eyes and appeared reluctant to let her pass out of his sight. It was not until Matthew had placed his hand on the small of her back and moved close that the other man released her.

"I have heard much about you, Miss Meriwether." Lady Patricia gave Trudy a generous smile. "And I see that rumor has not exaggerated for once. Sir Matthew"—she turned to him—"I do not believe I have ever heard a room go quite so silent as this one did when she entered. Have you?"

"No, my lady. But I am grateful to have you mention it, for I was beginning to think I had imagined the whole."

Trudy held her breath, assured she'd been discovered, but Lady Patricia merely sighed. "All the other young ladies will be in blackest despair. If I were you," she advised Matthew, "I should not let such a charmer out of my sight."

With those kind words and a smile, she waved them off and turned to greet her next guest, and Trudy could release her strangled breath.

"Marvelous advice," Matthew murmured behind her. He had bent to whisper into her ear. "My first order of business must be to secure your hand for the first two waltzes."

"Oh! But I meant to save them all for you!" Trudy protested, turning to face him.

Matthew stopped and smiled. "All of the waltzes?"

The startled look upon his face made her stomach flutter, though she wasn't sure why. "I had meant," she confessed with a shy sweep of her lashes, "to say all the *dances*."

A smile started on his lips. She could see he was trying to hide it, but unbridled amusement had lit his eyes. "I would be honored, of course. But do you

165

not think, perhaps, that such a high degree of particularity would seem . . . rather . . . particular?"

Trudy felt dimples burrowing deeply into her cheeks as a blush rose to heat them. "Would it? Why?"

"Because"—Matthew paused to clear his throat as he ushered her over to an alcove—"though you mustn't think I normally regard such mundane considerations—because, my dearest dear, the custom of these affairs usually dictates that a maiden lady shall limit each of her partners to no more than two dances—three if they are engaged."

"Oh—"

Matthew's next question cut her off before she could express her disappointment. "Would you truly reserve all your dances for me?"

"Of course. Are we not agreed that such foolish conventions are unworthy of our notice?"

"We are indeed. However, I am finding in myself an absurd desire to protect you from vicious tongues."

His serious tone took her aback. Trudy gazed into his searching eyes and felt something inside her diminish. "You needn't, you know," she said quietly. She rewarded him with her tenderest smile and thought she heard his sudden intake of breath. Matthew reached out a finger to caress her lower lip.

"Dunstone?" All around them the din had started to grow again. Now one insistent voice broke through it.

They both started, turning to find a gentleman at Trudy's side. "You do not mean to keep this young lady all to yourself tonight, I hope," he said, stepping forward to clap Matthew on the back.

"I had considered it," Matthew said ruefully. "Faye, I am forced to present Lord Cranleigh, who, I presume, has come to beg a dance. Lord Cranleigh, Miss Meriwether."

Trudy gave the young gentleman a glancing smile, but she clung to Matthew's arm. "Shall I have to—" she began, but before she could finish her plea, she was cut off by Matthew again.

"I am afraid so. Though not for the reason we discussed, but rather because, if you do not, we shall likely have a riot on our hands." He gestured behind her.

When she turned to look, she saw that a crowd of gentlemen had formed in their wake.

"But—" She nearly wilted at the sight of them. "What dances shall you and I have together?"

"All of the waltzes," Matthew said firmly and loudly to the gathering behind her. "I may lack your audacity, my dear, but I am no fool. Stay clear of the mistletoe, mind." He gave this warning to the men.

Just then a footman came up, and Matthew said to her, "Let me take your cloak." Before she could prevent him, he helped her off with it, and as the servant carried it away, Lord Cranleigh claimed her hand.

Trudy felt herself being swept away from Matthew to join in the dance that was forming. She thought of disappearing from the frightening scene, but her magic cloak was gone. Matthew's face was all alight with pride, and she could not bear to have his look erased. Besides, she realized as her nervous partner got up a harmless banter, she had often danced with other elves. Although the steps would be a bit different, the music was the same. It would not hurt her to take a few turns of the room on other men's arms.

She gave herself to the dance and tripped lightly about the room, pausing with a curtsy when the steps called for one. Every now and then, she glanced back to see Matthew, who was watching her with enjoyment.

At first his sanguine acceptance of these other men's claims made her wonder just how firmly his feelings were engaged. But then when she noticed that someone had offered him a chair, she recalled his recent illness, and she realized he could not dance the whole evening without doing himself harm. An abrupt awareness of his mortality seized her. It clamped on her heart with fear. Although he would live a great deal longer, Matthew would surely precede her to the grave by many years. Many decades, in fact. Perhaps by as long as a century.

And Trudy knew with an unquenchable pain that she would not want to live that long without Matthew.

Matthew had watched her glide about the room as if she floated on butterflies' wings, charming each of her partners in succession. As every head had turned to stare at her, he had not had to wonder how she managed it, for every time she merely glanced his way and smiled, he felt a pull so strong, he could hardly keep his seat. His impatience to hold her was becoming intolerable when he first saw her flag, as if some thought had swept all the joy from her.

He started to his feet, just as the music—most fortunately—stopped. He did not wait for her partner to return her to his side, for that was never likely to occur. Instead, he strode across the ballroom floor and claimed her right out from under the nose of her next supplicant.

"I believe this is a waltz," Matthew said with barely a glance at the other man, "and the waltzes are all mine."

Faye stepped into his arms, not even waiting for the music to start, and Matthew caught his breath. Her hair, which was as light and as feathery as down, tickled his chin; her phantom perfume teased his nostrils and made his head spin. While they waited for the other couples to form, Matthew closed his eyes and let a cornucopia of sensations take him.

Then the music started, and he was twirling her around the floor in perfect circular motion. Long out of practice, Matthew found that the steps came easily to him. He flowed with Faye. Although he led, his dancing skill seemed to emanate from her and her desires, as if she were a sorceress spinning him in a spell.

He might have waltzed on and on, enjoying this miraculous, almost spiritual sensation, but something about it made him feel uneasy. With his eyelids only half open, looking down into Faye's face, he could almost see Trudy gazing wistfully back up at him. He blinked hard once, then twice, and the illusion was gone.

"What is it, Matthew?"

Her gentle concern made him ache to hold her closer. Matthew wanted to fill his emptiness with her, but holding Faye like this was almost as disappointing as he had feared—she was almost lighter than air, not enough to fill his arms.

He tried to reassure her. "It is nothing. A passing thought, not worthy of comment."

But his smile must have been weak, for her dainty steps faltered. He caught her more securely, grasping her waist and hand in a tighter grip. Her body brushed against his, but still her substance failed to satisfy his growing needs.

Then, just as he thought he might burn from the frustration building inside him, his hand that held hers grew warm, and from that little bit of warmth, his whole arm began to hum. The humming spread from his shoulder to his chest, then to the rest of him, and he almost sighed aloud.

"Look up, Matthew." Faye's gaze tilted toward the ceiling, dragging his with it. They were spinning alone under the mistletoe.

Matthew almost felt that it had been she, and not he, who had brought them there, but with that warmth still humming inside him, he didn't care who'd been responsible. Still, with an affirmation of his masculine right, he determined to prolong this delicious moment as long as he could.

"Are you enjoying the ball?" He teased her by posing the trite question, for they had hardly spoken at all, so enthralled had he been.

"Oh, yes," she breathed happily. "It's all so warm, Matthew, so warm."

She glanced around them at the dancers, who were gaily laughing; at the fireplace, where a roaring Yule log burned; and at the children, who'd been roasting chestnuts over its flames. The rich, welcome smell of the nuts mixed with the wood smoke to fill the air with Christmas.

Her pleasure in these simple things nearly overwhelmed Matthew, who in his youth had always taken them for granted, if not despised them. Now, as he glanced around, holding her by the waist under the mistletoe, he saw that, indeed, there was something glorious in the warmth of human spirit in this room, and he felt more in charity with his own kind than he had in years.

But the heat inside him was building, too, as the dancers twirled about Faye and him where they'd paused. The sweet smells of apple and orange and evergreen wafted down from the rafters above.

"Matthew—" Faye tugged on both his sleeves, pulling herself deeper into his arms. "Don't you want to kiss me?"

He laughed, looking down into her enchanting face, where a touch of worry had wrinkled her perfect brow. His desire was suddenly inflamed by this hint of a flaw in a gem that was otherwise sublime.

"Yes, I want you," he said huskily, folding his arms so securely about her that her toes left the floor.

But when he would have kissed her as she'd wanted in the middle of the floor in front of the assembled company, she quickly struggled to get free. "No, not like that!" she said.

Matthew backed away, startled. The pairs who were dancing immediately behind him were forced to swerve, and the ladies squealed in fun. The gentlemen laughed in loud voices and called out encouragement to him.

"Faye? What the devil—" His enchantment had burst, but Matthew had to chuckle. Either that or strangle Faye.

But she looked so distressed, standing forlorn under the kissing bough, that he feared something was gravely wrong. He moved forward to take both her gloved hands in his.

Again that mysterious warmth invaded him from the fingers up.

"What is it, darling?" he asked, gently rubbing the backs of her hands with his thumbs.

"Like this," she whispered, refusing to answer him directly. Instead, she made him release her hands, only to take one of his up again.

Matthew let her do what she would, but her actions more than surprised him. For the first time in his adult life, he actually felt some embarrassment, for Faye was taking his first two fingers and slipping them inside the glove of her upheld hand.

Before Matthew could wonder what the company would make of this transgression, the pads of his fingertips brushed along her palm.

Their touch was electric. It sizzled along his arm, infecting the rest of his body so fast he gasped.

"Do you see?" she whispered mysteriously, her

green eyes bewitching him and beckoning him closer and closer, until their lips met.

And suddenly her substance, which he'd thought he'd found lacking, hit him in the chest like a blow from a club. It heated his blood and made his knees start to wobble. Matthew closed his eyes and gave himself up to their kiss.

Their kiss was far more than just a peck; it was much, much more than was improper; it was enough to send them both charging immediately into societal exile. But even though dim and vague recollections of propriety's mores hovered somewhere in the dark nether regions of his mind, he could not help himself or be distracted from this bliss.

Not until his fingers slipped inadvertently from her glove, and the bubble burst.

Matthew fought for breath. Faye's dreamy eyes flew open. They stood and stared at each other until a gentleman, dragging his giggling partner by the hand, tapped Matthew on the shoulder and begged him to make room under the bough.

Taking Faye by the hand—which he found to be trembling, else he might not have believed what had passed—Matthew pulled her to the edge of the dance floor, trying to collect himself. With heat seeping up from his neck, he struggled to find his voice, feeling as if he had just scaled the Mountains of the Moon.

One glance at his partner told him she had fared no better, for she appeared to be dazed. The eyes of the other guests followed them. Ladies had raised their fans to hide their whispers, which for once seemed to discompose Faye.

Matthew's head was still ringing from their deep encounter. He couldn't think of anything that would give him more pleasure than to propose to her right here and now, but that might rather wait until they were alone, and the night was still young, not even midnight. For all their talk of dancing every waltz together, they had only had the one, although . . . what a whirl it had been.

The exultation of their kiss had still not left Matthew, so he bent to whisper temptingly in her ear, "Shall we go?"

Faye fumbled shyly with her fan, but her eyes revealed a hint of secrets. "Very well," she said in a thrilling voice. "But you must let me get my cloak."

Chapter Eleven

*M*atthew fetched Trudy's cloak and would have led her immediately away from the party, but she asked if he might not wait a few minutes instead. The truth was that she had suddenly been beset by a cluster of worries too tangled to reason out, and she needed a moment of peace.

A small withdrawing room had been set aside for the ladies to use to freshen their toilette or to pin a sagging hem. Trudy started to enter it. Then, when no one was looking, she swept her cloak about her to make herself invisible. She did not want the stares or the attentions of other ladies to intrude on her painful thoughts.

She settled herself in a corner of the room away from three ingenues, who were giggling and gossiping while they combed one another's hair. Satisfied that none of them had seen her, Trudy folded her arms, sank her chin onto her chest, and struggled to hold back tears.

Tonight her wager with Francis would expire. Tonight was the night she had promised to lure Matthew into the mists. And tonight would, therefore, be the last time she would play at being human, an undertaking which had become much more than a game.

Trudy knew that she should be excited by the way Matthew had fallen into her spell on the ballroom floor, by the way he had abandoned himself so willingly to their kiss. And she was. The trouble was she wanted to repeat that kiss again and again for as long as she found it thrilling, but she was worried that would be impossible now.

There had been ingredients to that kiss she was not sure she could duplicate in elfland. Love and trust. Dedication and hope. Respect and free will. Each and every one of these principles had been part of it, but they would all disappear when Matthew learned she was an elf.

Oh, she might be able to hold him in thrall for long periods at a time. For a short while, she might even be able to make him forget how unmercifully she'd deceived him. But Trudy did not think for one moment that she would win Matthew's genuine love and respect once she had lured him into her world.

The sound of the three girls' voices raised in laughter reminded her that Matthew was waiting for her in the corridor. By now he would have conveyed her thanks to their hosts and would be growing impatient. He was a man who never liked to wait. But what could she do? She couldn't stay huddled in a withdrawing room until midnight and then fly away without him. She could never do anything so cruel to Matthew. Had he not warned her she had the power to wound his heart? If she decided not to take him into elfland, however, but to prolong her game, then things would not go much better for him.

At midnight she knew without a doubt that Francis would come to see just why she had not joined the family on the heath, and he would blow up a storm. If he saw her wearing Matthew's gloves, he would break into a fit. And if—as she was tempted so strongly to do—she decided to wear human clothes to trap herself in Matthew's world, all her magic would be gone and she would lose her family forever.

The very thought of losing her magic until Matthew chose to release her made her shake until her teeth clacked together. Much worse would be the fear she would constantly experience of wondering when Matthew would discover she was a creature without a soul. That thought, that shame, made her cringe inside her cloak.

Her worries unresolved, Trudy knew it was time to go, time to straighten her shoulders and face Matthew. There was nothing for it but to go through with her original plan, unless some brilliant inspiration could come to her at the last moment. Such things had happened to her before. Why did she doubt one would happen now?

She gathered her cloak about her just as the girls stopped their chatter and started from the room. She followed behind them so closely, they ought to have felt her breath upon their necks, especially when they stopped, blocking her passage through the door.

"There he is. Do you see?" The blondest of the

three ladies raised a hand to hide her lips while she whispered to her friends.

Mildly curious, Trudy glanced across the room and saw that the girl was pointing to Matthew. He was waiting for her, his tall, strong body draped in a drab greatcoat as he leaned against the wall. Trudy's heart filled with pride on remarking his air of casual grace and unwavering confidence.

"Oh, is that Sir Matthew?" the tallest girl was saying into the first girl's ear. "Now I see what you mean. He is sadly scarred, is he not?"

The first girl gave a shiver. "They say his face was pierced by a native's spear. Isn't he frightful?"

The brunette with bad teeth, the only one who'd been silent until now, spoke: "I don't think so at all. I think he looks very distinguished."

Trudy's heart, which had started to beat in defense of Matthew, began to slow before it was nearly whipped into a frenzy by the first girl's next remark.

"Distinguished?" The blond staged another great shudder. "Well, I certainly do not think so. I think he is rude. Did you notice how he refused to stand up with anyone except for that bold creature who came alone with him? Though I'm sure there were other girls waiting to dance. Not that I would want to dance with a man such as he, mind. I should rather die first. Although I suppose I might be persuaded to dance with him once out of charity. Do you know, they say he is a mere shadow of his former self, that he was at one time handsome? Well, I am certain that I cannot see it if he was."

This last statement was too much for Trudy, who

thought Matthew much the handsomest of all men, and the finest. She reached her hands out and gave the blond girl a wicked pinch.

Matthew, who had started to grow impatient, was searching for Faye with his eyes when he thought he spied Trudy instead, standing just outside the ladies' withdrawing room, close behind a group of girls. Her green eyes were sparkling with rage. Her pointed ears quivered. He blinked, but the vision stayed right before him, unlike the previous occasions this evening when he'd been able to shake off his delusions.

He must have come down with a fever for certain. He reached up to touch his forehead, but just then he thought he saw Trudy give one of the girls a pinch on the derriere.

As he started, she vanished as completely as if she'd never existed. He would have been positive he'd imagined the whole episode if the blond girl had not let out a sudden shriek.

"Eek!" She whipped around, but no one was there.

Matthew closed his eyes again and pressed them tight. When he opened them, Faye was emerging from the withdrawing room with a smirk upon her lips. The blond girl stared at her intently. A shade of resentment passed across her face, mixed with doubt, but Faye ignored her.

She crossed the corridor to join him. "Shall we go?" she asked with a smile.

"Y-e-es . . ." Matthew straightened from the wall, giving a push with one shoulder.

She paused to gaze up at him with a questioning

tilt to her chin. "You don't sound certain," she said. "Are you quite all right?"

"I'm perfectly ready to go," Matthew declared. "But I must be coming down with a fever again. I've been seeing things."

"What sort of things?"

"I hardly know—green felt—walls closing in—but there is one thing I must ask."

He turned her to face him, keeping hold of her upper arms, and thought he caught a guilty look. "Answer me truly, please. Did you or did you not just pinch that girl?"

Faye's green eyes grew round with fright. "Did you see me?"

"Yes. Should I assume this means you did it?"

She ignored his question and quickly posed one of her own. "What day were you born?" she asked, tapping her finger on his chest in an agitated fashion.

"April eighth—though what that is to the purpose, I cannot imagine."

"No! What day of the week?"

He drew back, more puzzled than ever by her earnest desire to know. He thought. "I believe it was on a Sunday," he said.

Faye shut her eyes, and her head fell back. He clasped her shoulders more tightly, afraid she was going to faint, but she only waved her head slowly from side to side.

"I had no earthly idea," she said despairingly. "If I had—" She broke off.

A vague misgiving seized Matthew. Memories of myths and folklore from his Scottish childhood reached out to worry him. But he pushed them away, instead giving Faye a little shake.

"Did you indeed pinch that girl?"

She sighed as if to lie would be worthless. "Yes, but she deserved it," Faye said firmly. "I should have pinched her much harder than I did, for I'm afraid she hardly felt it through her skirt."

Matthew gave a dumbfounded laugh. "You little imp! What on earth were you doing?"

"Defending you, of course. She said one of those things you hate—about how you're just a shadow of your former self—so I had to punish her. I think she was simply jealous because you didn't stand up with her for a reel."

Matthew had stopped laughing. He did not remember having mentioned those feelings to Faye. He could not imagine that he would have done so. He was always so careful to guard his feelings to himself.

Except with Trudy . . .

He looked at Faye now, and confusion clouded his head. He felt a frown crimp his forehead so hard it nearly hurt.

"What is it, Matthew?"

She was so tiny and so precious. Precocious, even. Almost like a child.

Or an elf.

He shook his head strongly, thinking this would never do. He must have experienced delirium again even to be entertaining such wild thoughts. And he must have told her how he felt in some moment when he had not been quite himself, like this evening.

"Matthew?" Her hand went to his forehead. She whispered, "Love?"

Her use of that word—so openly, so tenderly and fearlessly—caused a surge in his loins.

He would not be doubting her. He could not.

Matthew gently laid one of his hands over hers. "It's quite all right. But I suppose we should go before I embarrass us both. If you are ready now?"

Faye nodded, a strangely contrite look on her impish face. She must have thought he was disturbed about the girl, which he wasn't. The chit could go to perdition for all he cared.

To reassure Faye, he wrapped his arm about her as he led her from the house.

The wait for the carriage was not long. As soon as it came, Matthew gave the driver instructions to drive a few times around the park, before joining Faye inside. Then, at once possessing himself of her hand, he drew her onto his lap.

She came to him willingly enough. Although the light through the window was too dim for him to see her features, he sensed no strong reluctance. Her weight was so insubstantial as to disappoint him again, until she placed both hands upon his chest and he felt the resurgence of the hum he had felt upon the ballroom floor.

"Would you like to slip your fingers into my glove?" she whispered temptingly.

Her entreaty made his pulse leap with a mixture of bewilderment and desire. What kind of enchantress had he fallen in love with? Faye was no mere eccentric with an unhinged relative or two, she was a graceful witch who had turned his gift into some kind of fetish—and one in which he thoroughly believed. They were aptly paired, he and she. She, with her enchanting brand of insanity, and he, with his ravings and his persistent delusions.

"If you like," he whispered back, and in a moment his fingers were brushing the palms of one of her hands.

"Oh, God . . ." It was like nothing he had ever experienced. "Faye—" As he kissed her, succumbing to the softness of her lips and the magical smell of her breath, Matthew posed her a question. "Have you ever—would you ever—consider marriage?"

"I have not. But as to"—she kissed him softly again—"whether I would or not"—and again more tenderly—"that would depend entirely upon who the gentleman was."

They both deepened their kisses. If Faye had wanted to refuse him, surely she would not be kissing him with such abandon. Matthew felt the thrill of conquest, partnered by a deeper, more lasting sort of thrill, the profound generosity of love.

"Would you," he said, finally pausing to catch his breath, "take me for a husband?"

Faye fell silent. She was so still, she almost felt frozen in place, until she spoke. "Oh, Matthew . . ." She sighed, but her voice held a distinctly anguished note.

He felt her search for excuses and, with a sinking heart, thought that perhaps he should supply her with some. "I am neither a wealthy nor a healthy prospect. Is that it?"

"Oh no!" Real anguish entered her voice. "It's not you, Matthew. . . . It's me."

Before Matthew could challenge her for her meaning, the carriage jerked to a sudden halt, nearly throwing them on the floor. Matthew caught Faye as she tumbled from his lap.

"Driver! What is it?" he called out.

"Don't know, sir! The 'orses 'ave taken a fright and won't go for'ards. Herrup!"

They heard him trying to whip them up again, but though the carriage jerked and swayed, the animals had clearly balked.

"Let me see where we are," Matthew said to Faye. He peered out and saw that they were at the end of her street and that the driver had brought them home against his orders.

"The dolt!" Matthew bit back his curse and said instead, "We are at your house. Perhaps we should go inside to finish our discussion."

He still could not see Faye's face in the dark, but he heard her sigh as if her heart were breaking and felt her tuck a trembling hand inside his.

"What time is it, Matthew?" Her voice sounded tense and sad.

"I don't know." An uneasiness inspired by her tone seized him like a premonition. "About midnight, I suppose."

"That's what I thought."

She sighed again as he helped her from the carriage, and Matthew noticed that her face was whiter than usual, almost as if she were afraid of entering her own house. He hoped that his passion hadn't put that fearful expression on her countenance.

The fog that had covered Faye's house when

they'd left it had shifted enough to clear a pathway to the door. It still hovered, though, in wing-shaped wisps about the roof, giving Matthew the fanciful impression that a group of ghostly spirits had been left to guard its walls. Now, even as he reached in his greatcoat pocket for his purse, those wings seemed to change, growing larger, then rounder, until they sank from their own weight to envelop the house. The mist stretched in fingerlike tendrils as if to grasp anyone who might try to come in.

Matthew paid the driver while Faye waited, but when he turned, he saw her ahead of him moving toward the door. The portal's white paint still gleamed with an unnatural light, framing Faye's dainty figure in its glistening brilliance and bestowing on her black hair a bewitching glow. He felt a tug on his innards, pulling him toward her. The tug grew stronger and stronger with every step he took.

"Will you come with me, Matthew?" Faye's voice had grown more musical than ever, almost like sleigh bells in the wind. She extended one hand for him to take.

"Come with you?" Matthew repeated her words as if in a trance. The woods loomed darker about him. The mist curled in snakelike shapes around his ankles, giving him the eerie feeling that he would never reach her doorstep. The door was fading, fading into the mist.

"You mustn't come if you don't want to," she said, throwing a hand suddenly across her eyes. Now that he was nearer, he could see tears twinkling on her cheeks.

"What is it, darling?" Two more steps and he was nearly with her, though she seemed even farther away. "But, of course, I'll come with you. I love you, Faye."

"No, saab!"

Matthew heard Ahmad's cry ahead of him as he reached out one last time for Faye. "What—" He peered past her and saw his friend running out of the park.

Faye squealed and started to wrap her cloak about her, but Ahmad had moved too fast. He grabbed her by the wrists and dragged her to Matthew. "No, saab! You mustn't follow her, saab. It is all a trick. She is a jinni."

"Don't be ridiculous, man—" But even as his anger flared, a fearsome grip took hold of Matthew's stomach. Faye's house, which ought to have been in front of them, had suddenly disappeared. "That couldn't be."

"She is a jinni, saab. I have watched the house all evening. It is nothing but mist and magic, saab. She simply cast a spell."

Matthew looked down at Faye, struggling frantically in Ahmad's grip, and his delusions overwhelmed him again.

Trudy's pointed ears, which had haunted him all night, peeked out from beneath her shining hair. No longer did he see Faye in a fashionable velvet gown. Instead, she was an elf maid, dressed in a tunic of forest green. Her shoes were soft felt boots at the end of a pair of bare legs. Her whole costume had changed with the exception of one garment—the gloves he had bought for her himself.

"Let me go! Matthew, make him let me go!" The terror in her voice startled him awake. He staggered backward, but there was no porch on which to lean. No pillar. No house.

Then, another figure emerged from the mist—Francis, who hovered from a tree above them all. Fury, fright, and malignity glared out from beneath his grizzled brows. "Let me sister go, ye heathens!"

"This is a nightmare." Matthew felt himself beginning to shake. He covered both his eyes with his fingers and dug them deeply into his lids. He wished he had more fingers to block out Trudy's frightened cries. "I must be raving again. A raving lunatic."

"No, saab," his gentle friend spoke quickly. "You are not mad. I swear it. You must not think that of yourself."

Matthew could not trust Ahmad's voice. He knew he had to be insane if he believed in these delusions. He'd been troubled by visions all evening as in the past, except for the fact that he'd been performing perfectly well between them.

"I'm mad," he said again, despair overwhelming him. "I'm well and truly mad this time."

Trudy's shrieks stopped. He looked up, hoping that all his evil visions had flown away.

But she was still trapped in Ahmad's arms, and Francis still hovered angrily above them. The only difference was in Trudy's eyes.

She gazed at him regretfully, her expression full of love. "No, Matthew, dearest." His despair had turned her fright into anguish. "You are not feverish. I am an elf. You must believe."

Matthew wondered if he dared believe the evidence of his eyes. But he recalled the things that had worried him all evening—the sensation that the walls of her house were fading away into the woods, his impression that she had vanished from his sight, his suspicions of her uniqueness, and the quiet conviction, even though he had tried to dismiss it, that Faye was privy to his conversations with Trudy—and he had to believe. He could be mad, but there was too much logic to this madness.

Ahmad's enormous body with his turban and baggy pants dwarfed Trudy's fragile frame. The strong Pathan still held her in a cruel grip, though she had ceased her struggles to bend her head in shame. The gloves that Matthew had given her struck an incongruous note at the end of her felt-clad arms. The sight of those gloves awakened in him a different set of feelings.

Trudy had worn his gift when she could just as easily have conjured a pair for herself.

With a furious shake of his head, he refused to be drawn into speculation. He had been the object of some horrible, fantastic trick. Faye was not even human. If he had not witnessed so many times how vile and terrifying humans could be, the thought that he had fallen in love with some other creature might have repulsed him. As it was, his feelings were more simple than that. He thought his heart would break.

He straightened his back. "Let her go, Ahmad," he said, keeping his distance from Trudy. From somewhere in the tree, he thought he heard Francis sigh.

"But, saab—" Ahmad seemed loath to give up his

prize. "You might keep her for yourself. I thought you loved and wanted her."

"I did want her. But not like this. Not as my prisoner." He stared into his friend's pleading eyes. "You cannot have forgotten what that is like, Ahmad."

"No, saab." Ahmad's gaze fell to the ground. "I have not forgotten." Slowly, reluctantly, he released his grip on Trudy.

"But—damn you, heathens!" Francis called out from his safe perch. "You can't leave her trapped!"

"I've let her go, Francis." Matthew felt a weariness he had not known in many days, not since he'd first seen Trudy. But this complete exhaustion was more of the spirit than of his body.

"But them gloves! Ye've got to help her off with them gloves!"

"Why?" A tiny feeling—like hope—sparked in Matthew's chest, bringing his eyes to the ones he'd been avoiding.

Trudy was looking on him now with the sweetest mixture of sadness and longing. She approached him and put her hands in his.

"Because," she said gently, "when I wear this precious gift from you, I have no magic in my hands. What you've felt inside them is only me. The purest me."

A thickness entered Matthew's throat. "So that is why," he said, and went no further.

"Yes, that is why. But—" she added, and her low voice was full of regret. Her summer-sweet breath wafted near to tickle his nose. "Unless you remove them, I must live without magic in my hands for the rest of my life, for neither I nor my brother have the power to take them off."

"Take them off!" Francis shouted from his limb. "If ye don't take them off, I'll curse ye all to perdition!"

"That's quite enough from you, Francis." Matthew found his voice in anger. "You're an elf, not a god. And I don't need any curses from you to make up my mind."

As he'd spoken, he had begun to strip the gloves off Trudy's hands, and he did it roughly. He did not want to be tempted to put his fingers in them again, to feel that ecstasy of pairing with her or what she'd called her truest self. She could not be believed in this instance, or in any other, for she'd lied to him countless times.

He yanked them off, nearly making her cry out with his anger. Then, instead of flinging them, as he'd intended, he made her an ironic bow and offered them to her on upturned palms. "I believe I made you a gift of these," he said.

As Trudy slowly reached for them, tears built in her eyes. Matthew's response was automatic. He took her in his arms, all anger fled. He hugged her, and she tightly hugged him back, still feeling like little more than air. If he had wanted proof of her otherworldliness, this was surely it. He had only failed to recognize the sign.

"Trudy, no! Trudy, run!" Francis was leaping up and down on his limb.

"Shut up, Francis," Matthew said, wanting nothing to spoil this moment. He cradled Trudy's neck in his hands.

But Francis was frantic. He hopped and shrieked.

"Ahmad"—Matthew gestured to his friend, who waited patiently alert—"could you please do something to shut that gadfly up?"

"Yes, saab."

With no more words than that, Ahmad took out his long, dangerous knife and started to throw it up into the tree. Francis fled, shrieking like a monkey.

"Oh, I did love you, Matthew," Trudy sobbed into his chest. "I still do love you. I love you so much, I wanted you all for myself. But we can't be together in your world."

Despite all her tricks and her lies, Matthew knew he believed her. He had always been quick to assume the worst, to suspect treachery where none existed. Now when he was faced with the cruelest treachery of all, he found he still believed Trudy, could almost feel the quandary she'd been in.

"I know," was all he could manage to say.

Trudy raised her tear-stained face. She was still more beautiful to him than any human. "We could still be together, Matthew, if you would come with me. Of your own free will."

Her moist eyes begged him.

Matthew felt his heart being torn right out of his chest by her misery. It was so close to his own.

Her pull on him still was magical, although he sensed she was using none of her elfin wiles. This strong appeal was much more basic, much more real. It hurt much more.

"No, my darling"—he nearly choked—"I cannot come with you."

"But, Matthew"—she clutched his lapels—"you do

not know what elfland is like. I could make you happy there. I would feed you anything you wanted. I could show you any place you haven't seen. You would be healthy. I could help you live forever—or almost."

The picture she drew was one of paradise. Eternal life—or nearly so. Tremendous health and unending pleasure. Fabulous sights.

For one instant he was almost tempted. But what tempted him most were not all those things she'd described but Trudy herself.

"And what would happen," he asked her, "when you tired of me? Would you send me back to a world I would hardly know? Or would you leave me to wander, lost in the mist?"

"I would never tire of you, Matthew. I know that now, although I didn't at first. You and I are—" Suddenly and deeply distressed, she broke off.

"What are we, Trudy?" he asked. He knew what thought had caused her such disheartenment, so he prodded her gently. "Are we soul mates, you and I?"

She hung her head, giving it a little shake. "No. We're not that. We can never be that."

Matthew pressed her damp face to his chest and stroked her hair. A lump grew in his throat as he said, "I've seen what happens to men when they give up their souls, my dear. And I won't willingly lose mine. I thought I had once, and it almost ruined me."

"Oh, Matthew." She let his name out on a wail, and he thought his heart would break. If it hadn't already.

But he could not give up his spirit for a soulless creature, much as he loved her.

"It's time for you to go," he said, hugging her once, then putting her away from him. "Go back to your woods and your freedom."

Trudy fell back, stunned. He could see she had never thought it would come to a parting. Not really. Her elfin nature had not let her accept such a miserable end. Now she was paying the price for having such a free spirit.

And so was he.

"Come, Ahmad." Without a backward glance, Matthew called his friend, who hurried to his side. And for the first time in many days, Matthew needed the strength of Ahmad's arm to help him home.

Chapter Twelve

$\mathcal{T}$rudy stayed where she was, standing alone in the dark park surrounded by leafless trees and staring off into the bleak street where Matthew had disappeared. She stood and stood until her legs would no longer support her. Then she sank to the ground.

That was where Francis found her, in a heap, on the brown, frozen grass. He leapt right down from a tree, muttering curses about great, hairy heathens and all their progeny under his breath.

When Trudy didn't acknowledge his presence, he began to speak in a rallying tone. "Well, sister. That was a mighty close call, that was. And I was afeared for just a minute that ye'd really made a mess out o' things, getting yerself all mixed up with them humans. But I can see ye've been afrighted out of yer wits, so I won't scold ye like I ought."

Trudy sniffed. She didn't feel up to Francis's banter right now. She hoped if she remained silent, he would take himself off.

But her brother didn't take the hint. "I nearly thought ye had him there. Though for one minute I was worried he might talk ye into something else, which was why I stopped them horses. But, then, ye almost had him. He was afollowin' ye just as neat as punch, he was, and if it hadn't a'been for that heathenish friend of his, ye would've had him, I make no doubt."

"Ahmad's not a heathen," Trudy said with an angry sniff.

"Yes, he is. All them humans are heathens. Haven't I always told ye so?"

"Yes, but you're wrong." Trudy didn't know why she was wasting time arguing with Francis, for he would never believe her. But it made her feel better to defend Ahmad. "They're actually quite religious most of the time."

"Are they now?" His voice held a conciliatory note.

Trudy was stunned. That was the most sympathetic gesture her brother'd ever made, to let her think she'd convinced him of anything. Francis's unexpected kindness was one more burden than she could bear.

Trudy dropped her face into her hands and sobbed.

"Now, don't ye be carryin' on like that. The party's still going on over on the heath, and ye ought to come along. There's music and dancin' like ye've never seen. That's all ye need to cheer yerself up."

"No." She shook her head. "That won't be enough this time. I want Matthew."

"And ye would've had him, too, if ye hadn't carried on with them dangerous games o' yers." Francis was losing all patience with her. His tone was angry.

"Don't ye think I know?" Trudy almost yelled. "I

just couldn't help myself. That's why I did it. I couldn't do anything else, not after I saw him."

"But why, sister? The world's a beautiful place, and it's full of big, handsome men. And a lot o' them are much stupider than Sir Matthew, and they would've followed ye anywhere, as dumb as they are. Ye could've had yer pick o' them."

Trudy winced at his lack of understanding. "I didn't want a big, stupid oaf. I wanted Matthew, with all his greatness and his flaws."

"Well . . ." Francis seemed at a loss for words. He thought for a while before he said, "I guess I could try to trick him back for ye."

"No." Trudy was grateful to her brother, even if he couldn't understand. She tried wiping her tears.

"And why, girl? Yer not making any sense."

"Matthew doesn't want to live in our world, and I can't blame him. He'd lose his integrity."

"Integrity, shmegrity," Francis scoffed.

"You are not to scoff at Matthew!"

"All right, all right." He shrugged. "I suppose if ye have to be a human, he's a decent sort o' man."

"He's more than decent. Confess. You did like him!"

Francis rolled his eyes and said nothing, but Trudy knew he had liked Matthew. Francis would have been content for her if she had managed to lure a man as great as Matthew into the mists. He didn't wish for a big, bumbling oaf of a pet any more than she did.

"So, now what do we do?" he asked instead.

"There is nothing I can do. He doesn't want me."

"Sure he does. There's not a human alive who

wouldn't want me sister." He poked his chest with his thumb.

His pride failed to cheer her this time. "If Matthew had wanted me, then why did he let me go? Why didn't he even ask me if I wanted to stay with him?"

Francis chuckled. "Because he knew ye'd say no, that's why. And even human men have their pride."

"How do you know I'd have said no?"

Francis blanched. "Ye would have, Trudy." He darted an uneasy glance. "Wouldn't ye?"

Before she could answer, he answered for her. "Of course ye would have, so stop yer teasin'. Ye wouldn't want to live without yer magic now, would ye? Ye wouldn't want to live the way them humans do."

Disturbed by her silence, he started to pace back and forth in the park, waving his arms in wild circles about his head. "Oh, this is great," he shouted. "This is more than passing fine. Me own sister's gone soft in her head."

Trudy stayed quiet. She let Francis burn his anger out while he paced and stomped. The dry winter grass crackled under his feet until he'd worn a visible path about seven feet long.

"Tell me it ain't true," he finally begged her, coming to a stop beside her.

"I'm afraid it is," Trudy answered in a low, shameful voice.

"Well . . ." Francis's energy spent, his anger seemed to have vanished with it, but his eyes held a hint of sadness. "That do beat all. That's all I can say." He went on, "But I should have known. I should have known when ye were different, right from the cradle. I even heard our mother remark upon it a pair of times."

"On what?"

"Them inclinations of yers. They're not natural, that's what. That's why I've always tried to get ye to settle at home. I was always afeared that yer perverted nature would lead ye to do something foolish like this."

"What perverted nature? Why?"

Francis looked at her, his eyes full of warning, and placed his fists on his hips. "I've never told ye this, Trudy. I never did because I was afeared ye would get some sort o' bug in yer head, which I see ye have anyway, so I might as well tell ye now."

"Tell me what?"

"Ye'll recall all that talk about our ancestors? How one o' them was a prince, hunnerds o' years ago?"

She nodded, not sure where he was leading.

"Well." Francis sighed again and wiped the back of his neck, chagrin written all over his face. "I hate to be the bearer o' bad news, but it seems he was a human prince."

"He was?" This was interesting, but she did not get the point. "What does that have to do with me?"

"It means yer blood is tainted, ye thickhead. Same as mine, same as our mother's. Only neither Mother nor me ever showed any signs o' takin' after that side o' the family. When you did, which is what we always worried about, Mother and me."

"You mean, I might be human?"

"No, no! Nothing so weird as that. Only that ye

might be partly human, which would explain all yer strangest quirks."

"Well, thank you, Francis," Trudy said dryly. "I suppose you think that solves all my troubles."

"No, I don't! But—" He scratched his beard, then his head, then his beard again in frustration. "Ye've just got to tell me what ye want!" he said on an angry note.

"I think I want a soul."

"No, ye don't." Francis shook his head vehemently. "Nobody who's right in their mind would want anything of the kind."

"Well, I do."

Francis shrieked, "No, ye don't! Ye don't have the faintest little inkling o' what yer talkin' about. Souls are cumbersome, pesky things what nobody should want. They tie ye down, they take all yer fun away. . . ."

"Well . . . I still want one. I don't want Matthew to be disappointed when he holds me."

Francis sighed. Then he tore the peaked cap off his head and stomped on it until it was flat.

Trudy watched him and her heart reached out to him, for she could see he did love her in his own way. He could not bear to see her make a foolish mistake. She wished he knew how right her decision was for her.

By now Francis had picked up his hat, dusted it off, and pulled it back onto his head. He clapped the dust off his hands and said, "A soul now, is it. Well, that shouldn't be too hard."

"You don't think so?"

"Nah." He shrugged. "I'm sure there's hundreds of 'em just floatin' about, waitin' to be asked for."

"Francis, stop teasing me. Is there any way to get one?"

He thought a minute with his chin on his chest, his short, skinny arms folded, and his eyes screwed up. Trudy sent all her good feelings his way, for she was too upset to think for herself. If Francis couldn't think of any way to get her a soul, then she was doomed to a life without Matthew. She might hover around him, might watch his progress through the rest of his years. She might even visit him in his dreams. But she could not think of any greater torture than to watch him from a distance and not be any part of his life.

"I've got it," Francis said, making her start. "Or I think I have." He raised his eyes. "I've seen Old Christmas about this evening, and ye might ask him."

"Old Christmas?"

"Sure, and ye remember him. He's that old, gray-bearded bugger. The one what goes around on Christmas Eve bringin' pennies and such to them what believe in him."

"Pennies? And you think he could give me a soul?"

"Sure, and why not? They say he's a deep one, Old Christmas is. Ye might ask him for anything, and he'll do his best."

Trudy sighed. It didn't seem like much to go on, but she had to try. "Very well, then." She hugged her brother, even though he hated any demonstration of affection. "Thank you, Francis. You've been a great help."

His ears had turned a deep red, and so had his eyes. "Now, don't ye go blamin' me," he grumbled, "if ye get what ye asks for and then ye don't like it. Don't be expectin' me to get ye out o' this one, now. I've only done what ye asked."

"I agree," Trudy said. Then she released him, for he seemed all at once in a hurry to get away.

He did not fly off immediately, however, but instead dusted his hat again, as if he had not thoroughly dusted it already. With a lump growing painfully in her throat, Trudy waited patiently for whatever he might have to say. But when Francis spoke again, his words were nothing to the purpose.

"Well," he said, not meeting her eye but giving a sniff as he righted his hat. "I'd best be off. The Yule's not over yet, and I've got to get meself over to the heath. Give 'em the joy of the season and all that for ye, shall I?"

"Yes, please."

With a nod and no looks back, her brother took to the air. Trudy might have felt hurt that they'd said no good-byes, except that Francis had not threatened to wash his hands of her if she became a human. She suspected her brother's curiosity would not allow him to stay away from her for long.

After watching Francis go, she wondered how she would set about asking Old Christmas for anything. Since this was Christmas Eve, she could almost be certain he would be pulling his beard out with the number of errands he had to run in just one evening. She could hardly stop him in midflight to ask for anything so frivolous as a soul for herself when he had so many other, more desperate people to think about.

As Trudy pondered her dilemma, stories came out of her past, telling her what she must do. If she had a house, she would be expected to put out a shoe or a stocking for her Christmas gifts. Trudy thought of conjuring her magic house again, but that fantasy structure had never truly been her home. Her home was in a tree.

Well. If a tree was where Old Christmas would expect to find her, she had better settle for a tree.

Trudy was about to climb the nearest one, when something on the ground caught her eye. Investigating, she found it was the green dress she had bought to copy for the ball. It must have fallen from the bed in her room of illusion. It was still just as lovely as ever, though the press of damp leaves had left a brownish green stain just below the bodice.

If her Christmas wish was to come true, she would need all the real clothes she could get, and if it did not, she would need this souvenir of Matthew.

Tucking the gown under one arm, she climbed the tree and tried to settle herself down to sleep. She could use the ball gown for a fancy pillow. But her cloak?

Her habit had always been to wrap it about her, to make herself invisible to anyone who might wish her harm. The woods seemed empty tonight, but from experience Trudy knew better. All the spirits of the dead were alive on Christmas Eve. The witches and trolls would be roaming, ready to snatch up the unprotected.

But if Trudy wanted Old Christmas to find her,

she must not hide herself from him. Bravely she removed her cloak and draped it across a branch. She snuggled down onto her dress, hoping its soft pleats would help to conceal her from below.

Then she remembered what she had recalled about Old Christmas's practices, and with a jerk, she sat up to remove one of her shoes. Determined he should see it, she inched along a big, sound limb and wedged it down into a deep fork. She tested its snugness by bouncing up and down on the branch. Then, satisfied that the shoe wouldn't move, she crept back to her nest, muttering a prayer.

The velvet dress was soft. She hadn't thought she could sleep. But the emotional turns of the evening must have taken their toll, for as soon as her head touched down she was gone.

Along about dawn, a weary traveler passed aloft in the tree and spied an elf maid sleeping on a branch who was wearing only one shoe. It didn't take the traveler long to find its match.

What might have taken him much longer, if he had not been used to guessing people's secrets, would have been to discover what the pretty elf maid wished for herself. But years and years of looking into people's souls and peering into their hearts had made it easy for the old man to ferret out their desires. What was the one thing an elf maid didn't have, he asked himself, seeing her cloak laid purposely aside, that she couldn't conjure for herself? What would she put herself at such risk to gain?

Instead of moving to her shoe to place a soul in

it—a place it wouldn't do her any good, if she only knew—Father Christmas lowered himself silently to her branch and placed his knarled old hand upon her head. He spoke a few well-chosen words, for all that he'd seldom had occasion to use these particular ones, and felt the light of the Christmas spirit burning in his hand. It warmed him from his fingers to his toes—his only reward for all the miles and miles he covered at his age. It glowed on the elf maid's hair and disappeared, deep down inside her. It was not until the warmth of that heavenly glow had entirely disappeared that the old man withdrew his hand and likewise sought his rest.

Trudy awoke when the sun first cast its golden beam around the bend of the earth. She had slept soundly and peacefully, with something extraordinarily soft under her cheek. She sat up, wondering what it was, and all at once, her world turned upside down.

She started falling from the tree. Grasping for the limb, her hand found her pillow instead and dislodged it. She frantically called on her magic to stop her fall, but it did not.

Arms flailing, Trudy crashed through the leafless twigs and hit the ground with an "oof!" She felt as if all the stuffing had been knocked out of her body. Her back and elbows had been scraped, and a thick piece of cloth had fluttered over her face.

She lay there, blinded and stunned, for only a few seconds before recalling the wish she'd made on Christmas Eve. Had it worked? Did she really have a soul?

She'd never fallen from her branch before. Her head felt beaten like a drum. Her limbs felt heavier, too, as if cream had been ladled into them to weight her feet and hands. A new kind of spirit tingled inside her body.

She'd never been so completely terrified in all her life.

Gasping for breath, she tore at the material covering her eyes and discovered the green velvet gown, which must've fallen with her. And it was fortunate, too, for it was the only garment within sight.

Her magic cloak was gone. She looked up into the tree, but it wasn't there. Nothing was there, neither her cloak, nor the boot she'd wedged between the branches. The tree was as bare of clothing as she was herself.

Hastily, for she had no time to think of the consequences should she be mistaken, Trudy pulled the gown over her head. She struggled with its buttons, dismayed by the difficulty of such a simple task. Her fingers were so clumsy. She'd never had to use them this awkward way before. If something this simple was so difficult for her, how would she ever do anything more complex?

She found her arms were decorated with thin streaks of blood. The sight of her own blood nearly made her faint. Her pulse was racing, she trembled so mightily. She was almost afraid to stand up. But she could not stay seated in the park on a cold winter morning—Christmas morning—in a wrinkled ball dress with no shoes. Even though by this hour the witches and the dead would have retreated to their normal hiding places, a human or two could easily come along, and Trudy had no cloak with which to hide herself.

She had no choice but to go immediately to Matthew and to beg his forgiveness. But with a new kind of awareness that caused a catch in her throat, she realized that Matthew might not want her, no matter what Francis had said.

Francis. With a sudden ache, she remembered that she had not bid farewell to her brother. And without her magic, she had no way to find him if he chose not to show himself.

She mustn't think of her brother, though, or her Aunt Petunia or even that scapegrace Grace, or such thoughts would surely make her cry.

Trudy sprang to her feet and felt them sink with a thud to the ground, as if they were lead. It took her more than a few practice steps to become accustomed to this new weightiness. It wasn't that the feeling was unpleasant; it was simply new and bizarre. This realization gave her spirits a bit of a lift, until she found that the frozen grass and dry twigs she trod were pricking the tender soles of her feet like shards of glass. Every pebble on which she stepped bruised her arch like the meanest blow.

Yet, these same smarting feet would have to carry her the blocks and blocks to Matthew's house without her magic cloak. With anxious tears, Trudy wondered what sort of foolish mistake she'd made, wishing for a soul so far away from where he lived.

Deciding she had best not wait until the streets were filled with pedestrians and carriages, she wiped her tears with the back of one hand and started. Gilbert Street could be as much as two miles away.

Trudy found that this walk was nothing like the one she had taken so blithely the other morning. The pavement beneath her feet was so cold, it sent a chill right up her legs until her teeth were chattering, although fear might have played a part. The refuse covering the streets assailed her nostrils with the odor of rot. The feel of dirt between her toes made her shudder with distaste.

An occasional early riser crossed her path. Also, some who might never have found their beds or who had no bed at all stopped to watch her pass. As each man stared at her mussed gown and her dirty bare feet, she felt the shame of her appearance. With no cloak to hide her, she could do nothing but avoid their eyes, but still she felt their stares crawling like spiders on the back of her neck. Her own vulnerability made her want to flee, but she was not so sure her legs could run. Instead, she picked her way through the piles of rubbish left from last night's revelry and prayed that no friend of Matthew's would see her in this condition.

The sound of Christmas bells from the parish church hastened her pace even though her frozen lungs threatened to burst. Whatever it cost her, she must not be found on the London streets when the members of polite society started to emerge from their houses. Counting only six or seven blocks left to Matthew's lodgings, she started to sprint.

The sharp cobblestones made her wince with pain. Bitter wind stung her cheeks. Cold air burned her nose and the inside of her chest, but its dearth made her gasp. She could not manage to run the last block. She was too tired, too breathless, too much in pain.

Matthew's door in Gilbert Street shone like a hoard of gold at the end of a rainbow. The sight of it made her want to cry with relief, even though the possibility of his rejection brought tears of distress to her eyes.

What if Matthew couldn't forgive her for her deceit? What if he decided never to trust her with his heart again? What could she do—wish for Old Christmas to take her soul away next year? Though she hadn't had much time to get used to it, her soul already felt like an inseparable part of her being. Even as miserable as she was, losing her magic would be worth it if Matthew would love her.

Trudy raised trembling fingers to the door and knocked.

The noise sounded feeble. As feeble as her knees suddenly went when Ahmad's intimidating form filled the doorway. He glowered at her, unspoken curses rumbling in his throat. Trudy's heart plopped into her stomach. In her desperate haste, she had not thought what to do if Ahmad would not let her past.

Painful feelings pressed like a heavy grip on her chest. She could not speak for drawing breath.

Ahmad's face first wavered. Then it faded, to be replaced by swirling stars, spinning faster and faster until all was black.

Trudy felt a bounce. She was bouncing to the cadence of someone's step, moving higher and higher up some kind of hill. She was cradled in his arms like a newborn lamb. Her shepherd had a strong, broad chest and arms like the branches of a sturdy oak tree. But pain kept her eyes tightly shut against the light.

An ache was spreading from the soles of her frozen feet to her ankles and to her knees. Her back had begun to sting, right along with her arms. All she could do was let her head flop back and groan.

She felt her shepherd pause. Her body was shifted in his arms, and a door clicked open nearby.

"Saab!" It was Ahmad, calling from a region somewhere above her head; his voice was lowered with care. Warmed by the sound of his concern, she slept again.

"Faye!"

Matthew had been sitting up, staring at his fire all night, with the pair of gloves he had tried to give her clasped in his hands. He would have drunk himself into a numbing stupor if the past year or two spent in a state of frequent delusion had not made him value his mental clarity far too much—no matter how hurtful that clarity might be.

Trudy's deception, his pain upon its discovery, the tears that had bathed his chest—all these things pressed heavily on his heart. He had suffered before but never quite this deeply. The blows and wounds to his body, the scorching burn of others' scorn, even the knowledge of his own foolishness, which had been at fault, could not hurt him as much as his little elf maid had. She had wounded him in his deepest, most secret place. And yet he believed she had suffered as much, if not more than he.

To see her limp in Ahmad's arms made his pulse leap into his throat. What had she done to herself?

"Put her here," he said quickly, "on this sofa."

As Ahmad lowered his fragile bundle, Matthew took in Trudy's altered appearance. The ball gown she had worn last night was only half-fastened in back, revealing a large purple bruise upon her shoulder. The gown was stained and wrinkled. Her feet and legs were bare and covered with filth. Her tousled hair appeared to be full of tangles, and to Matthew's horror, he spied streaks of blood on her cheeks, mixed with tears.

"Faye." He fell to one knee and gently smoothed the hair away from her face with a trembling hand. "What's happened to you?"

Getting no response, he raised his eyes to Ahmad's face.

"I found her on the doorstep, saab," Ahmad said with a worried frown. "Could this be another trick?"

"I do not know." Seeing Trudy in this painful condition made Matthew grieve to say it, but after the events of the previous evening, he could do nothing else. "She looks hurt."

"I will fetch linens and water."

As soon as Ahmad left the room, Matthew hurried to the tray by his chair to pour a glass of his untouched brandy. Kneeling, he raised her head and tried to get her to take a few sips.

She coughed and spluttered. The warm amber liquid seemed to bring some color to her cheeks, though not the bloom that had been there before. She opened her eyes and saw him.

"Matthew." Moisture filled her eyes.

Before Matthew could ask her what had happened, Faye threw her arms about his neck, and instantly he felt a difference.

She felt so warm and soft and full, like a woman of real flesh and blood. If he had not known better, he would have believed her to be one.

"Matthew," she whispered again. "I asked Old Christmas for a soul and he gave me one. I can stay with you forever now, if you'll have me."

Fear, the fear of being tricked again, robbed him of speech. Could he believe her?

But as Matthew held her away, he caught a glimpse of her imperfections—a sickly pallor, small lines about the eyes he hadn't seen before—and he noticed that the intensity of her green eyes had faded. But even with these changes, she was still the most beautiful being he had ever seen.

"How long is forever?" he said, when he might have asked any number of things.

"For as long as we both shall live, but—" She swallowed, and Matthew could see the desperation in her eyes. "Oh, Matthew, I am ever so much older than you."

"It doesn't matter," he said, scooping her up into his arms to take her place on the sofa. She was still fragile, still smaller than other women, but she filled his arms as completely as she filled his heart, and he exulted in the feeling. "We shall be together just as long as we can."

"And you forgive me?"

"Of course. But how could you give up your magic, your very world, to be with me?"

"That's what Francis said, but I thought you would understand."

"I think I do." A barrier in his throat made it hard for him to speak. "I have been sitting here all night, wondering what kind of fool I was to let you go. But I would never have asked you to give up all those things you described, for I love you far too much."

He cradled her face tenderly with his hands. "Why did you, dearest? Why would you sacrifice the only life you've ever known?"

Her eyes bathed him with a gentle glow, and Matthew could see her new soul shining out from them. His heart skipped a beat.

"I couldn't live without you, Matthew," she said. "I didn't want to be an elf—my magic meant nothing—if I couldn't be with you."

A shuffling sound made them turn their heads toward the door. Ahmad appeared in the doorway, a blanket draped over one shoulder, a basin of water and strips of linen in his hands. He paused just inside the room to gaze back and forth from Matthew's face to Trudy's before permitting himself to smile.

"I have brought water for the memsaab," he said with a deep salaam. "And a blanket to wrap her in, for she will be cold."

"I was cold. Thank you, Ahmad"—Trudy struggled to straighten herself, but it was hard to sit with proper decorum in Matthew's lap—"but Matthew has warmed me up already."

"All the same"—Matthew took the bowl from

Ahmad and gestured for him to wrap the blanket around her shoulders—"we can't have you freezing to death. Not on Christmas. What would Francis have to say?"

His joke made Trudy bluster. Matthew ignored her indignation and set about wiping her face and hands with a damp cloth. But when he reached her legs and feet, he had to ask, "What happened to you anyway to cause so many scrapes?"

"I fell out of my tree this morning."

He paused in the act of wringing out his rag. His eyes met hers with the purest joy she had ever seen. Yet, all he said was, "I think we'll be having rather more fascinating conversations round the dinner table than typical newlyweds."

The sight of his overwhelming happiness was too much for Trudy's conscience. She had to make him see what she truly was. "But are you completely sure that you want me, Matthew?" she asked with a quiver in her voice. "For I don't know how to perform the slightest task. I know absolutely nothing about work, and when I told you I was an indifferent housekeeper, I was speaking the truth. I am next to useless without my magic."

Matthew looked at her, still smiling. "You speak Arabic, do you not?"

"I—" Trudy paused, uncertain. But when she checked, she found she had not lost that ability at least.

"Yes," she said, pleased. "I'm still fluent in many languages."

"Well, I should say that your particular talents will be of greater use to me than a little cooking and cleaning ever would. We shall leave those chores to someone else. I had far rather you helped me with the books I'll be writing, and I can tell you right now, you will make the most perfect travel companion a man could ever have."

Trudy would have protested her inadequacy longer, but Matthew turned to Ahmad and said, "Do you know, I am surprised you never suggested this particular course to me. We both should have known that I could only be happy married to an elf."

"That is very true, saab." Ahmad took the soiled cloth from Matthew's hands. "I hope you will forgive my omission to let me congratulate you both on your engagement."

"Of course." Matthew smiled at his friend. "And now, if you will excuse us, my fiancée and I have some important business to discuss."

Ahmad made them another deep salaam. "You do not think it would be wiser, Matthew saab, to have me stay for the sake of the memsaab's reputation?"

"I do not. Miss Meriwether and I are agreed that we shall not be ruled by intolerable conventions. Am I right, my darling?"

When Trudy saw the intensity of the desire burning in his gaze, she could do nothing but give up before she burst into flames herself. She smiled at him shyly and wound her arms about his neck. "Yes, that's true."

"So you see, Ahmad, that the matter is entirely out of your hands for the moment."

Ahmad grinned. "Yes, saab." He retreated to the door, then turned to wish them both a merry

Christmas before closing the door behind him without a sound.

So there ye have it—the terrible tragedy of what happened to me sister Trudy and the biggest scandal to be heard in elfland for many a year. Though, to hear me sister Trudy tell it, ye wouldn't think it was all that big a tragedy at all.

Trudy says that being human ain't half bad, but I think she's forgotten all the fun we used to have out on the heath when we was young, 'cause she's been so busylike. What with all that travelin' she and Sir Matthew do with that great big friend of his. I don't call that Ahmad a heathen anymore 'cause Trudy don't like it when I do, but he sure looks like a heathen to me, same as me brother-in-law.

But ye know what? I've did a fair bit o' travelin' meself now, I have. I had to do it, ye see, if I wanted to see me own nieces and nevvies. For the four of 'em, they're always gallivantin' about with their parents instead of stayin' at home like they should. But when I tried to tell Trudy that, she said she wanted to show them and Matthew all them places she'd been, only since humans do everything so slow, it takes 'em ever so long to get there, ye see.

So, I tries to bite me tongue where them kids are concerned, so Trudy'll let me see 'em when I want. Not that she could stop me or anything, but I likes to stay on the good side of me relatives, I guess. And Trudy didn't do so badly for herself, all things considered, though, as I've told her more than once, she *could've had them kids in elfland, same as not, and if she had, they'd've had pointed ears like me.*

But then, as I've told ye before, our Trudy always did like to do things her own way.